HAIRCUT AND HIGHLIGHTS

DAYTONA BEACH MYSTERIES
BOOK 1

JANIE OWENS

Copyright (C) 2022 Janie Owens

Layout design and Copyright (C) 2023 by Next Chapter

Published 2023 by Next Chapter

Edited by Tyler Colins

Cover art by Lordan June Pinote

This book is a work of fiction. Names, characters, places, and incidents are the product of the author's imagination or are used fictitiously. Any resemblance to actual events, locales, or persons, living or dead, is purely coincidental.

All rights reserved. No part of this book may be reproduced or transmitted in any form or by any means, electronic or mechanical, including photocopying, recording, or by any information storage and retrieval system, without the author's permission.

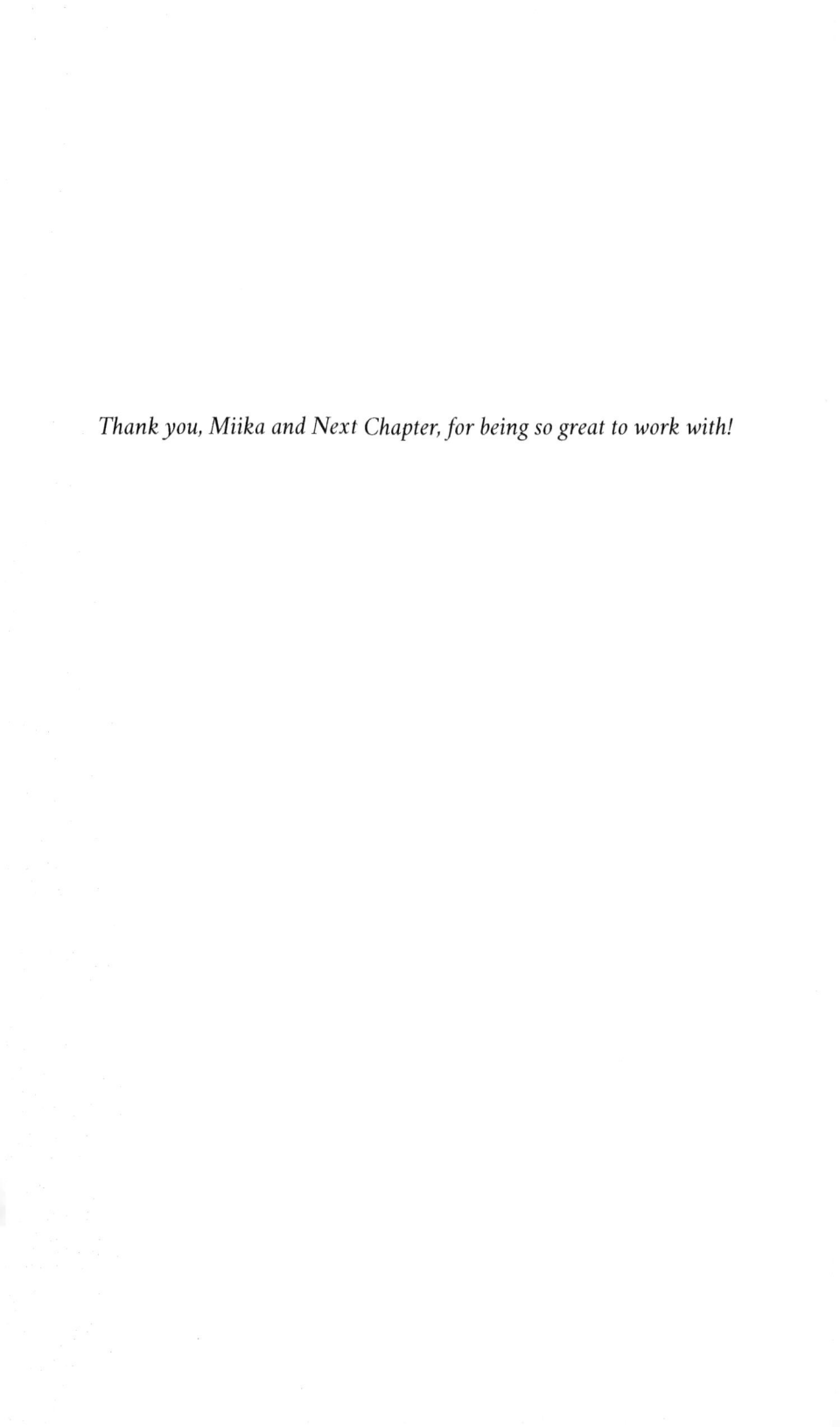

Thank you, Miika and Next Chapter, for being so great to work with!

ONE

HER HAND SHOOK SLIGHTLY as she stuck the key into the lock and pulled open the door. What had she done? Only invested into her heart and soul. Abby Bugsly stepped inside, glancing around the narrow room. Four booths, two on either side, were lined up in military order, the black chairs appearing to salute her arrival.

Abby tossed her keys on the curved desk that would meet customers. A collection of chairs was placed to the left with a round table in the center, sans magazines. Note to self: subscribe to magazines. She walked across the work floor to the back, noting the mirrors were perfect, nothing chipped. The stands attached to the wall underneath were in very good condition, which she had noticed when she inspected the property a week ago.

As she passed the two black shampoo sinks on the right, she made note of the storage room to the left, and then a white washer and dryer. On the other side, behind the shampoo bowls, was the pedicure room, and behind that, the breakroom for employees. The salon was well laid out, although small. And clean. That was important. No one wanted to get a haircut or their nails done in a shabby salon.

The downtown area had been on sorry times recently along Beach Street. Most of the building owners decided to place a new façade across all the businesses along the street and paint their buildings in different bright Florida colors. A good deal was promised on the rent for the first year to entice new businesses to occupy the buildings that were vacant. The rent was dirt cheap, so Abby had no problem with the price.

Back at the front again, she eyed the wall beside the desk. That was where her licenses would be displayed. But before that action, she had to start placing orders for supplies. She couldn't run a salon without hair color, shampoo and conditioner, and a multitude of other essentials. And employees. Abby pulled her cell from her purse, heaving that onto the desk. Some of the girls who used to work here were attempting to work from home she had been told. Abby had their numbers. Her intent was to contact each one to see if they had any interest in returning to the salon. She crossed her fingers and toes they were willing. She walked behind the desk and sat on the stool, preparing herself for a potential letdown, yet hopeful some were willing.

Abby hadn't lived in Daytona Beach, Florida, for several years. She'd had a stint at marriage and moved to Tampa. Moving to Tampa had been a disaster, along with the marriage. Daytona Beach was her hometown and where her heart was happiest. At first, she had stayed at a B&B that a friend of hers operated not far from the salon. Angie Barnes, now Forbes since her marriage, had offered her a room at a reduced rate until she found a place to live and landed a job. But when she discovered a salon among the cute shops along Beach Street, she decided to open her own. The bonus had been the availability of an apartment on the third floor of the same building. It didn't get better than that, living above her business.

HAIRCUT AND HIGHLIGHTS

"Hi, I'm Abby Bugsly and I am opening a salon on Beach Street, the one you worked at. I was given your name as someone who might be interested in returning." Abby paused for a response.

The woman at the other end of the conversation said she was pregnant and didn't want to stand on her feet all day.

"Oh, okay. Well, nice talking to you," Abby said. She punched in the numbers for the next person, receiving another disappointing answer. "Okay, number three, here we go."

She repeated her name and asked to speak to Sonia, since a man answered. When Sonia got on the line, her English was quite broken, making the conversation strained.

"Yes, I am located at the same salon you worked in. Uh-huh," Abby said as she listened carefully to the woman speak. "Oh, you are? That's wonderful. I plan to open in one week. Is that good for you?"

Apparently one week was perfect for Sonia and she was excited to return to her old job.

"Yippie!" Abby cried out loud. "I have one employee." And that was it. No one else on the list was available or willing to return. *Now what?*

Abby stuck her head out the door, looking both ways. She needed a cup of coffee. She locked the door and ventured down the street on a hunt to satisfy her craving. She glanced across the street at the fire station, followed by the yachts fastened to the dock. Such wealth! Way beyond her expectations. But the scene was nice to look at, and the breeze coming from the river was cool and refreshing.

"Hey, there," she heard and turned to see where the voice had come from.

An older woman dressed in clothes reminiscent of the 1960s was standing by the door to the next shop. The name of the place was Memories. "You renting that place?" she asked with a poke of her thumb in the direction of the salon.

"Yes, I am," Abby answered. "I'm Abby Bugsly."

"Nice to meet you. I'm Bobbi Bell," said the woman, coming closer. "This is my place. I sell everything that's old, cutesy, and makes you feel nostalgic. And some antiques. Real ones, not knockoffs."

"How nice. I'm a hairdresser looking for work, so I ended up opening this place," Abby said with a nod of her head toward her shop. "I need employees, though."

"I can put you in touch with someone. Her name's Ivy Snooks. My niece." Bobbi pulled out a pen and wrote the contact information on the back of her business card. "Real sweet kid."

"Thanks, I'll call her." Abby took the card, slipping it into her jeans. "I'm off for a cup of coffee."

"Two doors down is a deli. Coffee's pretty good there."

"Okay, I'll check it out." She took a few steps, then turned toward the other woman. "Nice to know you, Bobbi."

Bobbi nodded her red curly head and smiled.

Abby went inside and met some of the staff at the deli. Once she returned to her shop, she called the number Bobbi had given her. "Hi, yes, I'm Abby Bugsly. Your aunt gave me your number believing you were looking for a position in a salon." She listened intently as the obviously young woman on the other end of the line got excited at the prospect of working for her. "Yes, tomorrow will be fine to meet. Right next door to your aunt's place. Okay, goodbye." *Maybe* she had two employees.

Abby rose the next morning with a positive attitude, anticipating something good happening. *This will be a good day,* was her thought as she made her way to the kitchen. She poked the "on" button of the coffee maker, then did what she needed to do in the bathroom. Her kitchen ran into the living room, with a narrow hallway to the right where the bathroom was. The bedroom was across from there, with a smaller one next to the bathroom. She didn't need the second bedroom, but it came with the apartment. Each room was spacious, yet the place had a cozy vibe. So far, she liked living here. The rent was good, and the neighborhood was decent. She hoped to make friends with some of the shopkeepers.

She slipped on blue jeans and a blue tee, sliding her feet into brown sandals. That's when she caught sight of her toes and realized she needed a pedicure. A salon owner couldn't walk around with crummy feet. Bad advertising. Abby put on enough makeup to get by and pulled her blonde hair into a ponytail. After she stuck hoops into her ears, she eagerly poured a cup of coffee. A bagel with cream cheese was her breakfast. And coffee. Abby *loved* coffee. Then she went downstairs to her business. What a great commute!

Later, when Ivy opened the door to the salon, Abby was surprised she looked so young.

"You must be Ivy?"

"Uh, yes, that's me," she said with a nervous smile.

"I'm Abby. How old are you?"

"Nineteen."

Abby quickly realized that Ivy couldn't have much experience at that age. That meant she wouldn't have a following, which was important for a salon. She handed the young woman a clipboard with an application attached. "Please fill this out, Ivy. You can sit over there."

She nodded toward the waiting area. While Ivy filled out the form, Abby wondered about the other applicant. Would she have a following? She hadn't worked in this salon since it closed. Maybe she had kept her clientele by working from home. Abby could only hope.

"I'm done, Miss Abby." The chubby girl handed over the clipboard and waited while

Abby glanced at the application. It didn't take long because she didn't have any work history. "Let's sit down." Abby moved to one of the chairs. Ivy sat across from her. "So, you just graduated from beauty school, I see. You have not had any experience in a salon, correct?"

"No, ma'am." Ivy started chewing her lower lip, looking wide-eyed and innocent. Her red hair was too bright to be her natural color. It was common for girls going through beauty school to mess around with color. She had experimented, too, back then. "But I worked at the school, doing heads. I cut, colored. I was pretty good doing feet and hands. I did perms, too, but that's not my strong point."

"I don't think it starts out as anyone's strong suit. No worries." Abby looked at her round face, so full of hope. Should she take a chance with this young woman? If she didn't hire her, not only would she crush Ivy's hopes, she would anger Bobbi in all likelihood. So much for a friendship there.

"Here's the deal: you have no experience outside of school. Few salons will hire you being fresh out." Ivy's face crashed. Abby thought she might cry. "But I will. I will take you on as my apprentice."

Ivy's eyes bugged and she leaped to her feet, letting out a squeal of pleasure. Abby couldn't help but smile over the reaction. "Thank you, Miss Abby. I'll work hard."

"I know you will," she said, rising and embracing the girl. "Can you start next week?"

"I can start today."

Abby laughed. "Well, I don't have anything for you to do yet. My supplies are on order, but when they come in, you can help me set up. And I'll pay you. How's that?"

"Oh, that's wonderful! I can't wait."

Abby thought Ivy was going to jump up and down. "Okay, then. Go next door and give Bobbi the good news."

"Yes, ma'am." Ivy grabbed her backpack and ran to see her aunt, slamming the door.

Abby would have to get used to being called "ma'am." And "Miss Abby". When did she get so old? Apparently, to Ivy, forty-two *was* old.

TWO

Rose

ROSE TUMBLER ENTERED the facility begrudgingly. She didn't want to be here but was giving it a try. The homeless were encouraged to stay at the new shelter, but she rather liked sleeping outdoors, and that wasn't because she was a health nut or the outdoorsy type. No one told her what to do or when to do it. She was free to do as she pleased. In here, everyone was your boss.

"Any I.D.?" the stout woman asked from across the counter.

"Yeah." Rose pulled out her driver's license from a jean pocket and slid it over the counter to the woman, who wrote information on a form attached to a clipboard.

"This is your number. Don't lose it," she said, slapping down a laminated card in front of her. "You'll be in the second cot by the windows. Over there," she said, pointing in the proper direction. "The women's bath is that way, and the kitchen is down there." The woman continued to point.

"When do we eat?" Rose asked. She hadn't eaten all day, not that it was unusual.

HAIRCUT AND HIGHLIGHTS

"Six. You'll be evaluated in the morning. In the meantime, you can shower, eat dinner, and sleep here. Welcome!" Finally, she smiled, showing perfect teeth between her full lips.

Rose gave her a suspicious look, then nodded back. "Thanks."

Rose walked toward the room with cots. It was a long room, painted an appealing shade of blue. After she found her assigned cot, she pushed the trash bag that contained everything in her world underneath. Another woman came behind her, claiming the third cot. Rose hesitated to look at her. You never knew how people were going to respond when you looked at them. She didn't want any friends and she didn't want trouble. Immediately, the woman started talking to herself and complaining. Rose suspected she was a little off in the head. *Probably not on her meds.* That was common behavior among the homeless. A plus-size and dirty woman with an attitude was no one Rose wanted to know. To avoid conversation, she left the area.

"Rose?" The woman at the counter called to her. "Do you want to schedule your appointment for tomorrow?"

"Sure." She didn't want an appointment. All she really had in mind was a shower, hot meal, and a safe place to sleep. Then she'd be gone. But at this place, you could only stay if you were in their program to be rehabilitated. Other homeless were camped just past the gate. Maybe that was what she should have done. But then she'd not been offered a shower.

"Ten okay?" the woman asked.

"Um, yeah." She would have had breakfast by then and could make her escape. She gave the woman a slight smile, then moved to the showers.

"Hi, honey, would you like a shower?" The woman speaking was robust in build and had a pleasant expression.

Rose noticed her hair was pulled back in a low ponytail as she stood holding towels in her arms. "Yes, I would like that," Rose said.

"What size are you?" she asked, looking Rose up and down. "Don't look no bigger than a minute."

"Six? I think."

"Take these," she said, handing towels to her. "I'll get some clothes for you. Pick a stall. Shampoo and soap are in there."

Rose turned to the second stall and started undressing. Pretty soon the woman returned with clean jeans, a shirt, a sweater for cold nights, socks, and underwear. She hung everything on a hook inside the stall.

"You got everything you need?"

"I think so."

"Take your time. Dinner isn't till six." She left Rose to shower alone.

When the water cascaded over her head and body, Rose couldn't help but let out a long sigh. She hadn't had a shower since the one at the church downtown. That was a week ago, so she was rank. With her head sudsed up, she smiled over the pleasure of shampooing. The alluring scent of jasmine filtered into her nostrils. Such a trivial thing, but oh, such a wonderful experience.

When she finished, Rose put on clean clothes that fit pretty well. She stepped out to look at herself in the mirror hung over the sink. There she found combs wrapped in plastic, so she combed the knots out of her long brown hair and slid the comb into her back pocket. She actually looked presentable. Toothpaste and brushes were provided, so Rose brushed her teeth, then grabbed the toothpaste and brush for another time. As she left, Rose flung the towels into a bin. She hadn't felt this good since before she went homeless.

There weren't many women at the long table for dinner. Rose knew the shelter had only recently opened, so she thought that was the reason. Word hadn't gotten around yet. And then there was the fact that some homeless had no interest in staying here, regardless of showers and food, plus a cot. The meal was simple, Beefaroni and a salad. Of course, there was bread, and apple pie for dessert. Everything smelled terrific the moment she sat on the bench. She always loved Italian food. The scent of basil and oregano lifted her spirits every time.

When Rose returned to her assigned cot, she noticed the number one cot was occupied. Her desire was to avoid contact with any of the occupants, so she crawled into bed after removing her shirt and shoes. She chose to keep on the jeans in case she needed to make a quick escape, even though they were cumbersome under the covers. When Rose rolled on her side in the opposite direction of number three, she noticed the clean smell of the sheets under her nose. This was heaven. Rose went to sleep with a smile on her face.

Around two in the morning, according to the big clock hanging on the wall, Rose was awakened by a skirmish—right over her. Apparently, while she'd been sleeping, number three and number one had gotten into an argument. Over what, it didn't matter. All she knew was they were screaming and trying to slug each other while hovering dangerously above. She could see them grappling in the dim light and thought it was a matter of seconds before they collapsed on her.

A large man, followed by a woman, came flying into the room, calling out to them by name, not number three or number one. Rose scrunched herself tighter into the fetal position as the man and woman attempted to separate the women, one on either side of the cot. Once parted, the women were escorted from the room. Rose sat up, looking down the row of cots on either side. Only four others were occupied.

"Y'all almost got hit," twanged one woman.

Rose shook her head, then turned over for more sleep.

In the morning, Rose cleaned up and had breakfast. A different woman at the desk saw her walking around and called out to her. "You Rose Tumbler?"

"Yes."

"You have an appointment at ten with the counselor."

"I know."

"You'll be there?"

"Yes."

"Good for you." She returned to a stack of papers on the counter.

That was her cue to leave.

Rose gathered her things, pushing the toothpaste and brush into her bag. She twirled the plastic thingy around the edge of the bag and hoisted it. Now, if she could sneak out without being seen…

She peeked at the front desk and saw the new woman messing with papers. Rose kept her bag to the side of the door so the woman wouldn't see it. She walked to the water cooler, retrieved a cup, and filled it with water. While she drank, Rose eyed her surroundings. The front door was too close to the front desk, so it wasn't possible to escape unnoticed with that woman behind the counter.

After several minutes, a tall nondescript man came from another room to speak to the woman. "I need you to verify what happened last night."

"Okay." She left her post to follow the man back to the room. As soon as they were gone, Rose sprinted to the doorway, grabbed her trash bag, and was out the front door within seconds, marching past those who were camping outside the gates.

"Where ya going?" one asked.

"Back."

Rose made her way to the bus stop on Route 92 and waited for the next bus to roll by. She counted out some change for the fare. It wasn't long before a bus stopped to give her a lift downtown. Once seated, she thought about the shelter. It was pleasant enough, but it wasn't for her. She didn't want to settle back into the real world. Not yet anyway. Maybe someday. For now, she wanted to return to Beach Street. That was where she lived. On the streets with other homeless people, nestled into a storefront during the night.

THREE

"HOW MANY TIMES are you going to walk by and not stop in to say hi?"

The voice came from Abby's left side. She turned her head to see the sign that said Cat's Meow, with a formative black woman standing underneath, dressed in a long caftan in varying shades of yellow and orange.

"Oh, why hello. I didn't notice you there."

"Are you blind, honey? I'm big and brightly dressed. Even that blind homeless man across the street can see me standing here," she said with a smirk, then a laugh.

"I, well, I was in a daze, I guess. Just thinking," Abby said and smiled at the woman.

"Come on in here," she invited. Abby walked through her door.

"Oh, my, look at you," Abby said, glancing down to see a cat rubbing against her legs. He was a tabby with a loud purr. "Can I pet you?"

"If you don't, he'll not be happy," the woman said, adjusting her yellow turban with both hands.

Abby reached out to pet the feline. "How's the pretty boy?"

The cat responded with louder purrs.

"I'm Latisha Fairfax. I own this shop."

"Nice to meet you. I'm Abby Bugsly. I'm opening the salon a couple doors down," she said, offering her hand to the woman.

"Welcome to the neighborhood," Latisha said, pulling Abby into an embrace. "I do hugs, not handshakes."

Abby was all but smothered within the folds of the large woman. After the embrace ended, Abby asked what Cat's Meow was?

"A little shop catering to cats and dogs, but mostly cats. I also hold adoption opportunities monthly. Do you have a fur-baby?"

"Oh, no. I live alone."

"That's really sad. No one should live alone." Latisha pulled her head back to observe her more closely. Abby felt like she was being inspected. "I have three little ones that need a home. You'd be perfect for them."

Three? How could she go from none to three? "I-I don't think so. It's been a while since I had a cat. Or dog. Actually, I prefer dogs." She didn't really but thought that might dissuade Latisha in her pursuit.

"Hmm. You look like a cat lover," she said. "I know you love cats. I can feel it."

The way the woman's eyes were boring into her, Abby felt like Latisha could read her mind. "Maybe one?"

"One. Hmm. Follow me into the backroom." Latisha led the way to the far reaches of the shop.

Abby passed fluffy beds of varying sizes, shelves of bagged food, leashes for dogs and cats, several rows of toys, carriers, litter boxes and litter, and clothing. Latisha was well stocked for any conceivable need.

Latisha pulled back a cloth curtain to reveal the stock room. And a litter of kittens. They became quite vocal after seeing humans arriving. One of them was solid black, another a red tabby, and the third looked like it was Siamese, but obviously not a purebred.

"Oh, look at you," Abby said, reaching for the Siamese. "I love Siamese cats. I've had several."

"Take her."

"It's a her?"

"Yes."

"And I prefer females." Abby sighed. She knew she couldn't walk away from this adorable kitten. She looked at Latisha as she cuddled the fuzzy creature closer. "You got a deal."

"You're going to need some supplies," Latisha said as she walked toward the front of the store. She grabbed a litter box as she passed by, and then a bag of litter from the next section. She returned down the aisle, snatching up a scoop, kitten food, two dishes, and a small ball. "This will get you started."

Abby looked at Latisha with anxiety. "I sure didn't expect to do this today."

Latisha let out a loud, hearty laugh. "We never do." She bagged the articles for Abby.

"What do I owe you?" Abby asked, placing the kitten on the counter as she dug into her purse for a wallet.

Latisha gave her a price, then slashed it in half. "And the kitten is free."

"Latisha, that is too generous. I should pay you the full amount."

"Nope. Not happening." She gave Abby a toothy grin. "Welcome to the neighborhood."

Abby took the kitten and the supplies to her apartment. She stuffed the litter box into a corner of the bathroom, then poured litter in, and stashed the bag in the cabinet under the sink. Abby introduced the kitten to the litter box, then left it in the bathroom with the door closed. She didn't want it getting into trouble or harm.

As she arranged the cat food on a shelf and decided where to place the cat dishes, she asked herself what had possessed her to do such a thing? She didn't need a pet. She had a business to run. But she wouldn't be at the salon all day and night. There was plenty of time to spend with a kitten if she was being perfectly honest with herself. Besides, she didn't have friends since she had left the area, she wasn't in a relationship, so why not have a furry companion? Where was the harm?

Abby put food and water in the bathroom for the kitten, then returned to the salon. Sonia was due for her interview. When she entered the shop, Abby's first impression was of a gregarious woman.

"*Hola*," she said, waving her hand as she bounced in the door. Her hips were full under her jeans, her bosom more than ample in a snug red tee, and her overall fluid motion suggested a sensual woman.

"Hi," Abby said. "I'm Abby Bugsly."

"*Hola*, so pleased to meet you," she said in a thick accent. "Ooh, it hasn't changed," she said as her eyes cast around the interior.

"No, I thought it looked good as is, so I haven't touched anything."

"Ah, no need," she said with a wave of her hand.

Abby moved to a chair. "Let's sit down, okay?"

Sonia sat across from her, as had Ivy. "*Si.*"

Abby handed the clipboard with application to Sonia. "Please fill that out."

"*Si.*" Sonia began filling out the form. It didn't take long before she handed the clipboard to Abby.

Abby looked it over. "You have good credentials. I like that you have various skills, too. It's good to be diversified when business is slow."

"Ah, *si*. I like to do many things." Sonia sat erect with a smile on her face. *Good posture. Pretty lady. The men will like her.*

"I think you will be an asset to the salon," Abby said with

sincerity. "I plan to open next week. Is that okay with your schedule?"

"*Si, gracias.* I can let my clients know where to come."

"Perfect!" Abby had to ask a couple personal questions. "Are you married? Children?"

"No married. Divorced. Two children, but grown," she said, nodding her head. "You?"

"I'm divorced, too. No children, just a kitten." She chuckled. "That I actually acquired today. Do you know Latisha?"

"*Si*, two doors down. I know."

"Somehow I got talked into taking a kitten."

"Umm. Anyone else working here?" she asked abruptly.

"Other than myself, a sweet young woman fresh out of beauty school. Her name is Ivy."

Sonia rolled her eyes. "*Oy.*"

"I know, but I felt compelled to give her a start." She felt the need to explain.

Sonia raised both hands and bent them toward Abby at the wrist. "Your business." She stood to leave. "*Adios.*" And walked to the door, hips swaying. "See you next week."

After the door shut, Abby sat back in the chair. Obviously, Sonia did not approve of her hiring Ivy, a newbie. Well, the poor girl had to start somewhere. A bang at the door interrupted her thoughts, then a man carrying two boxes burst in.

"You Goldilocks?" he asked.

The question made her grin. "Well, yes and no. Goldilocks is the name of the salon, not me."

"Oh, sure. Where you want these?"

"Just toward the back," she said, waving her hand in the direction. "Leave everything on the floor, please."

The man laid the boxes down, then went back outside for more. When he was done bringing in boxes, he bid her a good day and left. Now, she had to unpack all the supplies and find everything a home. Abby reached into her pocket to pull out her phone. She dialed Ivy.

"Hi, Ivy. Can you come in tomorrow to help unload supplies?" Ivy answered yes, she would be there. "Wonderful. See you tomorrow."

Abby locked the salon and went upstairs to her apartment. After all, she had a little one to care for now. When she entered, Abby could hear the kitten squealing for attention. She opened the bathroom door, scooping the cream-colored feline into her arms. Barely was there any indication of color on the ears or tail yet, with no color on the face. Only big blue eyes stared at her.

"Oh, precious one. Don't cry. Mama's here now. Yes, I'm your new mommy," she said as she sat on the couch. The kitten purred like crazy and nuzzled into Abby's chest. "What am I going to name you?"

Many names entered her mind, but none stuck as being the right one. She couldn't tell by the absence of color if this was a chocolate or seal-point influence. Siamese didn't develop color on the tips until later, many not coming into full color until they were almost two years old. But because the kitten was showing a tiny bit of color at such a young age, it gave her the clue it might be seal point since they are darker.

"I'm going with you being seal point. So, I'm going to name you Seely."

The kitten made a "purp" sound, which Abby took as her agreement with the choice.

"Seely it is. Welcome home, Seely."

FOUR

ABBY ROLLED OVER IN BED, smacking her lips together. She discovered something stuck to her lip balm. Her fingers dislodged some hair. That's when she discovered Seely sleeping on the pillow, inches from her face.

"Bleh, hair. *Your* hair."

The kitten raised its head, looking at her with love in its blue eyes. "Purp."

"Purp yourself. Who said you could share my pillow?" Abby rolled onto her back. It had been some years since she had slept with a kitten. "Get used to the hair," she told herself.

This morning, Abby's usual routine was altered by Seely's arrival. The first thing she did was carry the kitten to the litter box and deposit her inside. Kittens were easy to train, but a little reinforcement never hurt. After all, she'd only been here one day. Then Abby did her normal bathroom duties. After, she walked to the kitchen to make coffee, with Seely following close behind. She prepared the coffeemaker and turned her attention to the feline, rubbing her ankles.

"I'll bet you're hungry. Okay, here comes breakfast." Abby

gave her a dollop of soft kitten food, then changed the water in her dish.

While the kitten ate and the coffee perked, she got herself ready for the day. Before leaving, she fixed herself yogurt with strawberries and toast.

Abby arrived intentionally earlier than she expected Ivy so she could get an idea where she wanted to display retail items and supplies. By the time Ivy arrived, she had opened all the boxes so she could see the contents.

"Hey," Ivy said from behind Abby.

"Oh! I didn't hear you come in," Abby said, turning from the box flaps she was spreading. "I need to get a bell to announce clients arriving."

"Good idea," Ivy said with a slight smile. "What do you want me to do?"

"See those containers on the counter above the shampoo bowls? Fill the white ones with shampoo, and the black ones with conditioner. The jugs are in those two boxes," she said, pointing at four boxes, each containing four jugs of shampoo or conditioner.

"Yes, ma'am." *There is that word again: ma'am.*

"You can call me Abby. You don't need to call me ma'am."

"Yes, ma'am, I mean, uh, Abby." She giggled.

Abby smiled to herself. At least the girl was respectful. "I'm going to furnish the display case. All these retail items need to be suggested to your clients. When you finish a shampoo, for instance, suggest they might want to purchase the shampoo and conditioner you just used."

"I see."

"When you style the hair, suggest whatever product you use."

"Okay."

"But not during every visit. Just do it at first, then periodically ask if they need any products," Abby said as she placed bottles and tubes on the glass shelving. She stood back to see if it looked inviting. "During the holidays, we'll have specials. And I'll sell you anything you like at a discount."

"Oh, that sounds good," Ivy said, tightening the pump applicator on a black container.

"Do you know how to clean a pedicure machine?" Abby asked.

"Yes, they taught us."

"Good. When you're done there, go into the pedi room, and clean the machines. It's hard to know when they were last used. I hope they still work."

Despite her concern and the long period of nonuse, the pedi machines both sprang into service. Ivy and Abby completed arranging the supplies in the supply room, wiped down the washer and dryer and the tables and stations for the hairdressers, then stood back to look at their work.

"I think we did a good job, don't you?" Abby asked, hands on her hips.

"Yes. It looks really nice." Ivy looked pleased with herself, her eyes smiling.

"It won't be long now till we open."

"I'm telling my friends to come in."

"Oh, good idea. We need the business. Now, if my sign arrives soon, that will help a lot." Abby threw her arm around Ivy's shoulders. "You're going to do just fine."

"Thank you. I'll try really hard," she answered, looking so sincere.

"I know you will." Abby liked Ivy. She was not sorry to take her on. "Let's go down the street and grab a bite. My treat."

"Okay. That would be nice."

The two sauntered to the small deli on the corner. As they passed Memories, both waved at Billi, and she waved back from inside her store. Next was Cat's Meow. They waved at Latisha, and she threw kisses at them. Dress 4 Success was the next shop, but Abby hadn't met the owner yet. Domino's Deli was

HAIRCUT AND HIGHLIGHTS

the last business on the block heading south. They walked in and took a seat. A young female server came over with water and utensils. She gave them menus and left.

"Have you eaten here before?" asked Abby.

"No, ma'am."

"Me either, except for coffee. The Greek salad sounds good to me. We could split a large one?"

"I'd like that. Let's do it." Ivy looked content to be sitting in a restaurant, looking around at the Italian-styled décor. She had such an innocent face, all pink and wide-eyed.

The server came over to take their orders and left again.

Abby wanted to know more about her new employee. "So, tell me, Ivy, are you still living at home?"

"Yes. With my mom. My dad left five years ago."

"That must have been hard on both of you."

"It was. Mom was really angry at him. He left us with only my mom's income, which wasn't much, so she had to get a second job." Ivy said everything thoughtfully, not looking directly at Abby. "She was always mad. Especially at me, like I had something to do with him leaving." She shrugged. "He yelled a lot, cussed. I didn't think he was a nice man. Him leaving was all right with me. But not her."

"Oh." Usually, children didn't like a parent to leave. "It sounds like your mother took her anger out on you."

"Yes. She surely did that," Ivy said with a sigh. "So, working will be nice, so I can stay away."

Abby suggested a way out. "Maybe you can save your money for your own apartment? Or get a roommate?"

"Mom wants me to turn over my paycheck to her so she can quit her second job." Ivy's expression clearly showed her discontent with that idea.

Abby did not comment. This wasn't her business. However, she didn't agree with the mother. Ivy's money was her money to do with as she pleased. Maybe pay her mother for rent and food, but not turn over the entire paycheck. That just felt wrong.

The server brought over one large Greek salad and two plates. Dividing a portion to their plates, they dug into the savory smells of oil, garlic, and cheese.

"This is delicious," Ivy said through her chewing, crunching a crouton. "Heavenly."

Abby grinned. She was glad Ivy was enjoying the salad so much.

"Are you married?" Ivy asked.

"No. I'm divorced."

"Dating?"

"Nope. Not dating either."

"You're so pretty. Are you picky?" Apparently, she couldn't understand why Abby wasn't dating.

Abby chuckled. "I'm discerning, but I wouldn't say I'm picky. I just got back in town after being away for a few years, so I haven't met many people yet."

"Oh. You'll get a date soon. The pretty ones always do," she said. It sounded like she was speaking from experience.

"Are you dating anyone?"

"No. I haven't dated much. I'm not pretty."

"I wouldn't say that. You have beautiful blue eyes, and your hair accentuates them." Ivy's only problem was that she still had baby fat clinging to her bones. Minus that, she'd be an attractive young woman. "Besides, you're young; you have plenty of time to date." Abby shot her an encouraging smile. "I'll work with you on your makeup, if you like."

"Awesome! I'd like that. I don't think I'm very good at makeup. Not yet."

"After we open, we'll do a makeover. How's that?"

"Great!"

FIVE

THE LETTERING FOR GOLDILOCKS' Salon glowed in shades of blue and gold above the entrance. Abby placed an open sign in the picture window beside the front door. Behind the other picture window, on the opposite side, were hair products for sale.

"We're ready for business," Abby said, looking from Ivy to Sonia.

"*Si*, I have customers coming today," Sonia said with a flourish of both hands. She cocked her hip in anticipation, her gold pants tightly gripping her body.

Each of the ladies had placed their personal styling equipment at their station. Ivy looked excited, while Sonia was impatient to get on with things. The first person in the door was one of Sonia's clients. She immediately went into animated conversation, escorting the client to her chair. Apparently, the client spoke Spanish because they both slid into a loud discussion, using words neither Ivy nor Abby understood.

Two men walked in next. Both were slender and tall, with clean-shaven faces and close haircuts. They were wearing sandals.

"May I help you?" Abby asked.

"Yes, we both want a pedicure," one said.

Abby looked at Ivy and raised her brows.

"I can do that."

Abby nodded at the young woman, and she sprang into action.

"Follow me, gentlemen," Ivy said, leading the way to the pedi room.

The morning dragged on because every woman who entered had an appointment with Sonia. "Lucky Sonia," Abby thought. *Where are the walk-ins?* Such a prime location should attract people.

The two men Ivy had been working on came from the pedi room wearing smiles. Abby looked at their feet as discreetly as she could. Their feet looked very good to her. As they left, one turned around and announced they would be back in a couple weeks.

Abby looked approvingly at Ivy. "Hey, your first regular clients! Good job."

Ivy smiled broadly. "They tipped good, too." She held up two ten-dollar bills.

"Excellent!" Abby knew the men probably wouldn't tip that well every time. She felt they were being kind to a young girl starting out, which was nice of them.

Abby heard the new bell jingle and turned to see a woman with hair as white as white could be, pulled into a French twist. The purse hanging from her wrist was leather and a designer brand for sure. "May I help you?"

"I'd like my hair washed and styled like this," she said, indicating with her hand the current updo.

"Of course, come right this way," Abby said. She led the older woman to a shampoo chair.

"Are you sure you can handle a French twist?" the woman asked.

"Quite certain."

"Because some can't get it tight enough so it stays in place a full week," she said as Abby fastened a cape over her clothing.

"Not a problem. I've done many French twists. I'm Abby, the owner of this salon," she said as the woman lowered her head into the cutout section of the bowl.

"I'm Mrs. York. If you do a good job, I'll be a regular," the woman stated, closing her eyes as the water gushed over her head. "My girl died suddenly, and I didn't want to go all the way to the mall to find another stylist. I saw your sign and took a chance."

As Abby ran her fingertips over the woman's scalp, building suds, she knew she had a customer. French twists were her specialty for the older crowd. Never had she had a displeased client. Abby smiled as she worked.

As the day wore on, quite a few women discovered her salon had opened. Some came in for a business card so they could call for an appointment later, others requested immediate service. One particular woman caused a stir when she entered. She was quite tall and like a beacon with bright red hair piled up on top. She peered around and spotted Abby.

"You look like you're in charge," she said.

"Yes, I'm the owner. My name is Abby."

"I'm Ruby Moskowitz. I live in a condo on the beach side, and I used to come here to see Janet."

"Oh, yes, Janet. I'm sorry, but she doesn't work here anymore. She's pregnant."

"Oh, too bad. Well, you know what I mean," Ruby said. "Are you available?"

"Soon as I finish this lady," she said, indicating the woman in her chair. "Just have a seat over there."

Ruby walked to a vacant chair, folding herself into it. Ivy and Abby exchanged looks without saying a word. She appeared ancient, judging by the jowls and wrinkles on her face, yet walked like a model. When Abby finished her client, she asked Ruby to come over to her chair.

"Oh, my bones," Ruby said as she sat back in the chair. "I guess at ninety-four I should just be glad to be alive."

"You're *ninety-four?*" Abby asked.

"Yes, dear. And I got married this year, but I'm not telling you how many marriages that makes."

Ivy caught herself before she giggled out loud.

"You certainly hold yourself well," Abby said, flattering the client.

"It's all in the attitude."

"What do you want me to do to your hair?" Abby asked.

"More of the same. Just wash it and put it back to normal."

"Will do." She began to dismantle the stack of hair in her hands.

For their first day open, Abby was pleased with her success, as was Ivy. The young woman smiled from ear to ear as she counted her tips after they closed.

"I can't believe I made this much in tips!"

"You did a good job for your first day in a salon. I'll work with you on some tricks when doing haircuts."

"I'd appreciate that, Miss Abby." The glow warming her full face reinforced Abby's decision to hire a newbie. Ivy was eager to learn and had basic talent. It would be a pleasure to share her years of experience with this young woman.

"I done," Sonia announced, ruffling up her hair with both hands. "Ah, my hair a mess. Needs a cut."

"I'll cut your hair for you, Sonia," Ivy volunteered sweetly.

Sonia gave her a horrified expression, obviously not wanting a novice to touch her locks. "No, dear. I cut my hair." She spun away to the supply room.

Abby looked at Ivy. "Most hairstylists are particular about their hair. She's one of them."

Ivy nodded her understanding.

HAIRCUT AND HIGHLIGHTS

When Sonia came out of the supply room, she carried her purse and her expensive blow dryer. *"Mañana."*

They said goodbye to Sonia. Abby looked at Ivy. "Why don't you go home? You've had a good first day. Go rest."

Ivy smiled brightly. "Okay. Mama will be surprised to see me."

"Tell her what a good job you did for your first day."

"I will. Thank you, Miss Abby." The appreciation shone in her eyes as she turned toward the supply room.

Abby began counting out the cash in the drawer and balanced the credit card figures with the register's sales receipts. After Ivy left, she went to the door to lock up and saw a homeless woman standing outside. She was dressed in shorts and a tee, typical Florida clothing, and carried a blanket over one arm and a garbage bag in the other hand. Her brown hair hung limply past her shoulders. The woman appeared younger than she, and probably would be attractive with a decent haircut.

Abby raised her hand and nodded. The woman smiled back cautiously, then walked on. *Interesting.* She couldn't explain why she felt an attraction to this homeless woman. There was something about her, as if she had known her at some time in her life. Was that even possible? Abby knew homeless people traveled to Florida from other states, especially during the colder months. This woman could be from Anywhere, USA. Yet she was familiar.

After placing the money in a bank bag, Abby gathered her purse and walked upstairs to her apartment. She noticed a man in a uniform entering the back apartment before she reached the landing. She wasn't sure what the uniform represented, but she thought it might be worn by a fireman. Abby didn't get a good look before he was inside. All she could say if asked to describe him was that he was tall with blonde hair, well built, and wore a dark blue uniform.

Seely met her at the door, meowing a greeting.

"My little munchkin," Abby said, leaning over to pet the kitten. "You came to mama to say hi? Precious little girl." And the motor started loudly; the kitten's purring was on high drive.

Abby picked up the kitten and walked into the kitchen, slinging her purse toward the couch, and then the bank bag. "Dinner? Is it dinner time?"

She fixed the kitten a meal, then took the purse and bank bag into her bedroom while Seely ate. Next, she scooped the litter box, the fumes making her turn her head away. "Ugh."

By the time she came back to the kitchen, Seely was finished with dinner and wanted attention, so she climbed up Abby's jeans, her tiny, piercing claws easily penetrating the fabric. "Yikes! Easy! Ow!"

Abby snatched her away from her thigh, enfolding her little body into her arms. "I don't believe in declawing, it's cruel, but I know why people do it. *Owie*. Let's not do that on my furniture, okay?" She placed Seely on one of the three bar stools next to the tall counter that separated the kitchen from the living room so she could make herself dinner. A bag of premixed salad seemed like a good idea, with a chicken breast sliced on top. She popped the chicken into the microwave, appreciating the convenience it provided. When the chicken was cooked, she sliced it over the salad and poured on ranch dressing. As she sat beside Seely, she ate dinner and thought about her circumstances.

She had to return to Daytona Beach. She hadn't enjoyed living in Tampa. Too much traffic, too busy, and always hotter than here. Besides, she was born in Daytona Beach. Even though both her parents were gone, it was preferable to live here than anywhere near her ex-husband. She couldn't stomach that idea. She had spent far too many years in a tortured marriage. Enough was enough. After she left him, she had tried to avoid a chance run in, which had proven difficult, so she escaped to Daytona Beach. Heaven on earth for her. If she never

HAIRCUT AND HIGHLIGHTS

saw her drunken husband again, she would rejoice. Any love she held for him had dissolved with the flow of whiskey.

Her parents had brought Abby up right, taking her to church, Sunday school, vacation Bible school, the whole works. She lived a good life—a life filled with service and helping others—until she met the smooth-talking Eric Straus. He had completely swept her off her feet. She remembered the promises he had made, the stories he'd told her about how successful he was.

None of it had been true.

He'd lied in the beginning of their relationship and all the way to the end. Abby came to the conclusion that he was a pathological liar. He lived to lie. There was no hope for their marriage. So, even though she didn't believe in divorce, she'd found herself in a situation where she had no choice. The only bright side in their marriage had been their inability to have children. She didn't want to bring children into such a negative marriage or have them go through their parents' divorce. So, it had turned out to be a blessing that Eric was incapable of fathering children as a result of his drinking.

Abby looked down at the furry feline that had decided to climb up her shirt. "No, no, not a good idea." She removed her from the shirt, bringing her around to cuddle. "It's just you and me, Seely."

Abby was an only child, and both her parents were gone. Since there were no other living relatives, her statement to the kitten was quite accurate. Everything had suddenly changed in her life the night she had gone to dinner with her parents to one of their favorite seafood restaurants. On the ride home, their vehicle had been involved in a terrible accident.

She shuddered at the memory of the mangled mess she'd viewed from the police cruiser. The front end, so twisted and smashed, had been struck by a semitruck going the wrong way on the bridge. The only saving grace was the slow speed the vehicles had been traveling, which saved Abby because she was riding in the backseat. She'd been untouched, but her parents were pronounced dead at the scene. She'd been twenty-two at the time.

Tears gathered in her eyes over the saddest memory she carried. "Just you and me."

SIX

ABBY HAD ALMOST REACHED the entrance to the deli when a blonde woman came out of a shop called Dress 4 Success. A slender figure dressed in black, she was very attractive, with hair that bounced around her shoulders. Abby smiled at her.

"Hey, I know who you are," the woman declared, pointing at Abby. "You just opened that salon, didn't you?"

"Yes, I did. Are you the owner here?" They were both walking in the same direction.

"Yes, this is my place. Let's get coffee and go inside. I'll show you around," the blonde said. "My name is Hillary Loughty."

"I'm Abby Bugsly," she said, stepping into the deli after Hillary opened the door.

"Two coffees," Hillary told the server behind the counter. "My treat," she said, turning to Abby.

"Thank you."

The server handed over the coffees.

"Sugar, sweetener, cream, whatever you want." Hillary pointed a red fingernail to the right side of the counter, where all the items she mentioned were displayed.

They added their preferences, snapped the covers closed,

and left with their drinks. Again, Hillary held the door for Abby as they entered Dress 4 Success. Abby took a sweeping look around. She saw racks of clothing of every description; pants hung together, blouses and casual tops hung separately, and dresses filled the entire length of the right-side wall. Shoes were displayed farther down, as well as undergarments. At the left front area was a sparkly display of jewelry.

"You are well stocked," Abby said, genuinely impressed.

"The people I cater to usually have very little to wear that is acceptable for job interviews and to wear once they land a job. I supply everything they need from jewelry to underwear. And I give them all my personal styling advice." Her red lips smiled, insinuating she had expertise in that area.

"That's a wonderful service you provide."

"I like to think so. The women need help getting back on their feet again after a divorce, or possibly having run from a nasty domestic situation," she said, sipping her coffee. "Local agencies help fund the operation and I accept donations."

"I am glad such a service is available. My heart goes out to women in need." Abby couldn't help but think of the homeless woman she saw the previous evening. "I have seen some homeless people around this area."

"Um, yes, we have a few. Most stay out near the jail, at a shelter. Others prefer to sleep in alleys or anything vacant." She shuddered. "Can't imagine living like that."

"Me either. All of them come from somewhere. I can't help but wonder what their stories are … what horrible circumstance brought them to the street." Abby shook her head.

Changing the subject, Hillary asked, "And where are you from?"

"Right here in Daytona Beach. I've been living in Tampa for a while, but after my divorce, I wanted to return to what I know." Abby took several sips of coffee.

"I'm from New York State, but I love it here. No snow to

deal with. But the humidity is a killer. Wrecks the hair." Hillary gave a slight smile before she continued. "I'm divorced, too, and decided that I didn't have to live in the cold anymore. I don't have children, so why not go someplace that is a vacation destination? So, I picked up and moved to Florida. I've been here five years."

"Good for you," Abby said. "It looks like you've done well for yourself."

"Oh, I'm not rolling in it, but I'm comfortable enough. And I'm happy."

"Well, that's everything, in my opinion."

"Yes, it really is."

"I've enjoyed our chat and becoming acquainted, but I need to get over to the salon," Abby said as she stood. "We'll have to eat out sometime soon."

"That would be great. Bye, Abby."

When she returned to the salon, Ivy was busy washing hair and Sonia was cutting hair. Everything looked peaceful and under control. Her appointment with Mrs. York was in a few minutes. She sat in the customer's chair, smelling the wafting shampoo and hair product scents.

"Abby," Sonia said, "I walk by the shop before you open. There was a woman sleeping at the entrance."

"Really?"

"I see her around sometimes. She homeless." Sonia kept snipping.

Abby wondered if this was the woman she had waved to.

"You not let the homeless do that, right?"

Abby didn't know how to answer, and then Mrs. York entered, looking flustered.

"Hi, Mrs. York," Abby said, getting out of the chair.

"Yes, hello to you, too." The older woman sat in the chair stiffly. "I have a crick in my neck." She rubbed her neck.

"Oh, dear, that's not good. I have a remedy." Abby went to

the pedi room and pulled out one of the hot towels they used for pedicures, then wrapped it around the woman's neck. "Why don't you rest for a few minutes before we get started?"

"Oh, that feels good. Yes, I'll just sit here and close my eyes."

Abby left her alone.

When she returned, Mrs. York was in better spirits, especially after Abby gave her a treat by massaging her neck. A trip to the shampoo bowl followed, then back to Abby's chair. Mrs. York gave Abby a big smile. "You are a gem. The pain is gone, thanks to you."

"I'm so glad. Now, just relax into the chair while I fix your hair."

The rest of the day ran smoothly, with Abby solving all the problems that came along.

"Are you leaving early?" Abby asked, seeing Sonia packing up her station.

"*Si.* I have *mucho* date. Appointments done."

"That's nice." Abby hadn't been on a date since she left Eric, and that was almost a year ago.

"I have a date, too," Ivy announced with a big smile.

"Really? Well, that *is* nice."

"We went to the same college."

"Daytona State?"

"Yes. He was studying computer maintenance while I was doing beauty school." Ivy was holding her backpack, obviously planning to leave right after Sonia. "I didn't think he liked me then. But I guess he did ... or does now."

"That's great. Have a good time," Abby said, really meaning it. The girl deserved to have a boyfriend. It didn't appear she'd had one before. She needed to grow up and not be under her mother's thumb. "What did your mother say?"

"She doesn't know. And I don't plan to tell her," Ivy said, looking slightly defiant. "She'd tell me I can't go. So, I'm not telling her."

HAIRCUT AND HIGHLIGHTS

"I see. Where does she think you're going?"

"Over to a friend's house."

Abby hesitated to advise the girl. It wasn't her business, after all. But put in the mother's shoes, she would want to know where her daughter was. "Don't you think you should let your mother know? If something happened to you, she should know where you are."

"Nah. Nothing's going to happen. And she'd stop me from going. I can't tell her."

Abby put her two hands in the air in surrender mode. "Whatever you think best. You are an adult."

"Yes, but my mother doesn't treat me like one."

Abby understood the look of determination on Ivy's face. "Have a good time."

"Oh, I will." Her blue eyes sparkled with excitement.

Abby said a silent prayer for Ivy's protection.

After closing the salon, Abby walked by Memories and glanced in to see if Bobbi was inside. She saw the woman wave and beckon her to come in.

"I wondered if you were open," Abby said, poking in her head.

"I'm really closed, I haven't gotten over there to turn the sign around," Bobbi said, standing behind her register. "Would you mind?"

"Of course." Abby turned the sign so "Closed" faced the public.

"Have a seat over there." She pointed at a wooden rocker. "That chair's pretty sturdy. Not that you're a heavyweight. Geez, you're a rail."

"I don't know about that." Abby was slender, but a rail? She didn't see herself that way.

"So, how's the salon business going?" she asked before coming from behind the counter to join Abby.

"Pretty well, all things considered. Three of us handle the

customers. That's enough right now because we're taking off slowly, as word gets around. But I'm satisfied."

"That's good to hear. The salon should do well with your location. Everyone passes by Beach Street. There's a B&B on the next block, so visitors should find this salon convenient."

"I hope so. I know the owner of the B&B," Abby said. "She's the mother of the daughter running the B&B. Her mother is Rachel Barnes, and the daughter is Angie Forbes. Sweet girl."

"Speaking of sweet girls, how is Ivy doing?" Bobbi asked.

"I think she's doing really well, especially since she's so green. They can't teach everything in beauty school. And experience is necessary to gain confidence in interacting with customers. They aren't all nice and polite," Abby chuckled. "She needs experience to achieve the perfect cut. Or perm. Or color. There's so much to learn."

Bobbi nodded. "I want her to succeed. She needs to get away from that woman she calls mother."

"Oh? That bad?"

"Worse. She's my sister-in-law, and we have never gotten along. Nasty woman. Cusses and drinks too much. Ivy needs to be on her own." Bobbi fell silent before she added the clincher. "Or at least away from her mother. She beats up on Ivy, too."

Bobbi's words rattled inside Abby like dice in a cup. She knew what it was like to live in fear of a slap or shove. Even a punch.

"Maybe she'll be able to move out now by having an income."

"Not if the mother gets her meat hooks on her paycheck." Bobbi gave Abby a look that said there were still challenges ahead for the young woman. "I'm also concerned because she's been so protected. She doesn't know how to fend for herself. She's scared to speak up. I'm not sure she even knows how to balance a checkbook or the proper way to write a check."

"I can work with her on those things." Abby reached out a

hand and placed it on Bobbi's arm. "I'm fond of Ivy. I'll watch out for her and try to guide her."

Immediately, Bobbi's eyes moistened. "Thank you. I knew you were a good person. I could just tell."

Abby smiled. "It's how I believe. I'm a Christian, so I try to help people when I can."

"Well, bless your heart."

SEVEN

WHEN ABBY CAME around the corner of the building, she saw a woman sitting in the doorway of her salon. It was the same homeless woman she had seen a week ago, and no doubt the same person Sonia had seen sleeping in the doorway.

"Oh, well, hello," Abby said, looking down where the woman had made herself comfortable during the night. A large garbage bag beside her was partially open, and she had a blanket on top of her legs. Immediately, she jumped to her feet and began pushing things into the bag.

"I-I'm sorry. I'll move. Sorry," she said as she bent to stuff articles away.

"It's okay," Abby said gently. "I don't mind if you sleep here during the night. Really, it's okay."

Through dirty brown strands, she peered at Abby, not sure how to respond. A blue knit hat, despite the warm weather, topped her head. It had seen better days, the fabric appearing pilled and holey. Abby wanted to rip the dirty thing off her head.

"My name is Abby. This is my business," she said and waited for a reply.

The woman looked warily at her before she spoke. "Rose."

"That's such a pretty name."

"My mother's name, too," she answered with a shrug.

"Well, Rose, if you'd ever like a haircut, I'd be happy to give you one. My treat." Abby looked into her face, trying to read her thoughts. Then the thought occurred that she might have insulted the woman. "It's not charity. I give free haircuts sometimes to people. It's just something I do." That wasn't actually true. This would be the first since opening the salon.

Rose nodded her head. "Okay."

"Any time you want one, come by," she said encouragingly. For some reason, she wanted to help Rose. She couldn't explain her feelings, just that the desire was there.

"Okay." Rose picked up her bag and swung around, bumping it into Sonia, who had just rounded the corner.

"Watch where you're going," Sonia snarled, then shook herself. "Ick. Trashy."

Abby unlocked the door, holding it for Sonia. "You have something against homeless people?" she asked as the woman walked in.

Sonia let out a stream of words in Spanish that Abby didn't understand. "Dirty," she understood.

"I'm sure she cleans up nicely," Abby said.

"Don't come near me, umm," Sonia said, waving her hands. "No like."

"You don't know her, so how can you like or dislike her?" Abby walked around the counter to open the register.

"She homeless. Dir-ty." Sonia emphasized the last syllable in the word.

"She's still a human being."

"Ick. No like."

Ivy walked in, slightly late. "Sorry I'm late," she said with her head down. Her overly red hair fell into her face.

"Not by much. No worry."

When Ivy slung her hair off her face, Abby immediately noticed a bruise near one eyebrow. "What happened to your face?"

Ivy hung her head quickly. "I-I, uh…"

"Walk into door?" asked Sonia with a smirk.

"Ivy, tell me what happened?" Abby crossed the room to Ivy's station and stood in front of the girl, waiting.

"Okay. My mother hit me." She raised her head so her bruise could be clearly seen.

"Why? Why did she hit you?"

"She caught me coming home from my date. She got mad 'cause I didn't tell her about the date. Then she called me names. And hit me."

Abby didn't know what to say, dropping her head until she spoke. "That's not acceptable behavior. Your mother has to realize that you are an adult who's almost twenty. But you also have to be honest with her and tell her about your dates."

"I did that once, and she beat me. I couldn't go out because I had bruises all over. Couldn't hide them, there were so many," she said quietly, pulling the side of her hair to cover the current bruise.

"Do you have more bruises now?"

"Yes." Ivy turned around and lifted her shirt to reveal a series of bruises on her back.

"Oh, Ivy. You *have* to get out of there."

"I don't have anywhere to go."

"What about your Aunt Bobbi? Could she take you in?"

"I don't know. I never asked her."

"Go next door and talk to her. Show her all your bruises."

"Yes, ma'am."

Abby plopped into Ivy's chair, letting out a long sigh.

"Um. Not good," Sonia said as she plugged in her blow dryer.

"No, it's not."

A half hour later, Ivy returned.

"Come back here with me," Abby said as she walked through the salon towards the employee area behind the pedi room. Once there, where no one else could hear them, Abby asked what Bobbi had said.

"She called my mother and yelled at her. They had a big fight," Ivy replied, sitting in one of the chairs by the table.

"So, what happened then?"

"Aunt Bobbi hung up on her. I could hear Mama yelling over the phone … until she was cut off. Now, I'm afraid to go home 'cause she's going to be *really* mad at me. She's going to be waiting by the door with something to hit me with."

"Oh, brother. This is bad," Abby frowned. "You can't go there by yourself."

"I know. I think Aunt Bobbi will go with me so I can get some things."

"Doesn't your mother work two jobs?"

"Yes."

"Then go when she's not home."

"That would be eleven o'clock at night. I don't know if Aunt Bobbi will go with me at that time."

"Ask her."

"Okay."

By the end of the day, Ivy had worked out an arrangement with her aunt to get all her clothes—and whatever personal items she could collect—out of the house while her mother was at work. Then, she was to stay with Bobbi until other arrangements could be made for housing.

Abby was relieved that Ivy would spend the night in safety. It broke her heart to know this sweet girl was being abused by her mother, of all people. But tonight, she would be safe from swinging fists and angry words. *Thank you, God.*

After Abby closed the salon, Ivy walked next door to go home with her aunt.

The next morning, Abby was eager to hear what happened with Ivy and Bobbi. Ivy had hardly walked in the door before Abby pummeled her with questions.

"We waited until Mama had gone to work, then drove over to get my things. She'd left a nasty note for me, asking where I was and why I missed dinner. She said we'd have a talk when she got home." Ivy slung her backpack on the chair at her station. "That meant I was in for another beating."

Sonia muttered something in Spanish as she stood at her station, listening.

"But she didn't come home before you left?"

"No, we got out of there without seeing her."

"Did you leave her a note, telling her where you are?"

"Aunt Bobbi left a note saying I was with her and not to worry. Also, said Mama wasn't to come by her house or she'd call the cops." Sad, Ivy sat in her chair after tossing the backpack on the floor. "I don't think she'll come by."

"All of that sounds good. I'm sorry it has come to this, but it was necessary."

"Yeah, I guess so."

Abby reached out and hugged Ivy. "It will be okay. No worries."

Sonia came over and hugged Ivy, too. The threesome, with their arms wrapped around one another, let out a group sigh, and then began their day.

EIGHT

"HEY," called Latisha. "Come on in here."

Abby turned toward Cat's Meow and passed in front of the owner as she entered. "Hi," she said with a big smile.

"So, how's the kitten? I thought you'd come over and give details." Latisha walked back to a chair.

"I'm sorry. I've been so busy. But to answer your question, she's just wonderful. Her name is Seely, and she's full of energy and sharp claws." Abby sat in the other chair across from Latisha. "She is such a delight to have around. I'm so glad you pushed her on me."

"Pushed? Humph. Didn't take much for you to grab that kitten and run, as I remember."

Abby laughed. "Maybe so."

"It sounds like she's getting used to her new home. I knew you would love having her."

"I certainly do. After a full day at the salon, it's nice to have some company that doesn't require a lot of talking. Although I do carry on a conversation with Seely. And she talks back."

Latisha laughed.

"Do you know a homeless woman hanging around here? Her name is Rose, in her forties, I would guess, brown hair. Carries a large trash bag?" she asked, changing the subject.

"I've seen her. Caught her sleeping at my door a month ago."

"Me, too. But I told her I didn't mind."

"Hmm, not good for business."

"Well, not during business hours. But during the night, I don't care."

Latisha eyed her. "I don't encourage that sort. They steal, trash the area. I don't need that attitude."

"No one does, but we can help, don't you think?"

"Help? What are ya gonna do? Give them a place to live? Hand over money? Cook them dinner?"

Abby bowed her head, then looked at Latisha. "I believe in helping people in need."

"They don't want your help."

"Not everyone out there wants to live on the street."

"Maybe."

"I think there's hope for Rose. I want to help her."

Latisha shook her head. "You're choice. Don't involve me."

Abby stared in disbelief at the woman. Latisha stood. "Well, I have to get supplies out."

"Okay. I need to get to the salon. Bye."

Abby walked out of Cat's Meow, feeling like she'd been dismissed.

It was a slow day. Not many appointments for Sonia or Abby, and few walk-ins for Ivy. As they sat around in their chairs, the ladies heard a soft knock at the door and looked at the door, seeing through the glass that it was Rose standing on the other side.

Abby walked to the door and opened it. "Hi, Rose. You didn't have to knock. Come in." Abby could almost feel Sonia cringe behind her.

Rose lowered her head and spoke softly. "Could you wash my hair? Please?"

"Of course, Rose." Abby led the woman to the shampoo bowls, noticing she was not wearing the knit hat. "Put your bag on the floor. Now, sit back and relax."

Abby gathered the brown hair into her hands and fanned it into the bowl. It was thin at the ends, she noticed, and smelled dirty, yet not as dirty as she had anticipated. She lathered Rose's head twice to get it clean, then used conditioner to smooth out her hair. While she worked, Abby was surprised to see there were few lines on the woman's face. Living outside had not caused her to age prematurely. Yet.

"Okay, Rose, come this way to my chair," she said after wrapping the woman's head in a towel.

Rose picked up her bag and deposited it by the chair.

Standing behind Rose, Abby combed the hair straight down, then handled her hair to determine what to do with it. "Rose, do you have any preference?"

"Not really. I'm just happy to get clean hair," she said, looking at herself in the mirror. "Sheesh, I'm a wreck to look at." Rose wore jeans and a tee, which seemed to be what the homeless wore, from Abby's observations. There were some spots on both, but Rose didn't have body odor.

"Do you want me to cut it a lot or just get the dead ends off?" Abby had ideas how to style her hair, but maybe Rose had some, too.

"What do *you* think?"

"I think we should cut it to here," Abby said, aligning her hands beside Rose's chin. "That would be easy for you to care for. A sleek bob."

"Okay."

Abby gathered portions of hair into clips, then scissored away any length below the chin. As she unclipped sections and applied the scissors to the next layer, Rose was able to get an idea of what the end result would look like.

Sonia stayed across the room, watching. Ivy stood nearby watching intently as Abby worked her magic. She did a final detailing of Rose's ends, then blew the hair dry, facing the woman away from the mirror. When she finished, Abby spun Rose around to view herself.

Rose's mouth fell open. "That's me?"

"That's you, kiddo." Her hair shined and moved softly as she turned different ways. The cut flattered her face shape perfectly.

"It's been a while since I looked even close to this. And then, I didn't look this good." The woman stood and turned around to face Abby. "Thank you so much. I would hug you, but I'm not clean."

Abby reached out and hugged Rose close enough to smell the hair products. "I think you look great. I'm glad I could do this for you."

"Thank you." She looked at Ivy and Sonia. Ivy was beaming at her, and Sonia looked stupefied. "She does good work, huh?" They nodded. "I can't pay you," she said, looking at Abby.

"I don't want any pay. This is my gift to you."

Rose reached for the bag and smiled as she moved to leave. "Bye."

"Goodbye, Rose," they all said.

Abby could feel her heart swell. She felt so blessed to be able to serve someone in need. Maybe giving Rose a new look would encourage her to help herself. How that could occur, she did not know.

Hillary marched into the salon, breaking into her thoughts. "Hey, how ya doing?"

"Terrific."

"I'd like to invite you to a gathering after work," she said, fluffing out her hair with both hands. "Some of us meet down at

HAIRCUT AND HIGHLIGHTS

the deli every so often to yak and talk about our businesses. You know all the girls, I'm sure."

"That sounds nice. Thanks for inviting me."

"Just come any time after you leave here."

"Will do."

A couple hours later, Abby locked up and walked to the deli. She noticed busses roaring by, emitting ugly gas fumes. The pigeons she encountered on the sidewalk appeared oblivious to the stench, each pecking around for food. One of the yachts sounded its horn, adding to the noise of the late day traffic. The sun was drawing down as she walked into the deli and spotted Latisha, Hillary and Bobbi sitting at a round table in the corner. Everyone greeted her enthusiastically as she took a chair.

"Welcome," Hillary said, "to the Chat."

"Thanks." Looking at Bobbi, a thought occurred to her. "Where is Ivy?"

"Her mother picked her up on the corner. Ivy wanted to visit her, so I thought enough time had passed that she would be safe." Bobbi stirred her iced tea with a straw as she talked.

"Yes, it's been a couple weeks. She should be over her anger by now."

"Bobbi told me about Ivy getting beaten. Pathetic example of a mother," Hillary said with a shake of her head.

"When I grew up, my mother took a switch to all of us kids, but never laid hands on us," Latisha said. "Umph, sorry woman, beating her kid like that."

"Hopefully, that is over. Now, I have to find her a more permanent residence." Bobbi sighed. "So far, no luck."

"What about girlfriends? She could have a roommate," Abby suggested.

"She doesn't have any real friends. Ivy was so sheltered, she really doesn't know anyone to room with," Bobbi said. "I don't particularly want her living with me and my husband forever. A little while, till she gets on her feet, that's fine, but not for years."

"We'll have to keep an eye out for a roommate for Ivy." Hillary waved her hand in the air at the server. "I'm going to order something. I'm starved."

"Me, too," Latisha said.

"I have to feed a husband, so I'll pass," Bobbi said.

"I have to feed a kitten soon, so I'll pass, too," Abby grinned.

"I heard you did the homeless woman's hair," Hillary said.

"Yes. I wanted to help her. I figured looking better might give her some inspiration to get off the street."

"Humph," Latisha muttered. "I'll believe it when I see it."

"If she gets a job interview, I'll donate some clothes," Hillary offered. "It's the least I can do."

"Thanks, Hillary, I'll take you up on that," Abby said. "Now, if I can get her interested in working …"

"Ha!" Latisha snorted.

Abby gave Latisha a look that said, what's your problem? "Maybe all she needs is a helping hand?"

"All you can do is try, right?" Hillary smiled. "I like your style."

"Thanks."

Latisha said nothing and looked away.

A good looking man dressed in a navy-colored police uniform walked in the door. He was tall with wide shoulders and a sizable chest. White teeth shone against his tanned face when he smiled.

"Ladies, nice to see you," he said, nodding at them as he walked by. His blue eyes danced below heavy dark brows when his glance fell on Abby.

She looked up at him, wearing a deer-caught-in-the-headlights expression.

HAIRCUT AND HIGHLIGHTS

"Who is that?" she asked her companions as the man stood at the counter to order.

Hillary was first to educate her. "*That* is Jack Pardon. He's a sergeant in the Daytona Police force. Nice guy. Comes in here frequently. Checks on us when he's on duty. I think he likes to make sure we ladies are safe."

"He's quite handsome. I always like a man with dark hair and blue eyes," Abby said, feeling mesmerized.

"Ump, look, she's smitten," said Latisha.

Abby's cheeks reddened. "Don't be silly. I'm just admiring the territory."

"He's worth admiring," Bobbi stated. "But I'm married."

"And you aren't," said Hillary to Abby. "Want me to introduce you?"

"I, well … it s-seems—"

"Hey, Jack!" Hillary called as he walked by. He turned toward her. "This is Abby Bugsly. She just opened the salon a few doors down."

"Hi," Abby said weakly.

"Oh, I wondered who had opened up there," he smiled. "I've been meaning to stop in. I like to know who's in my neighborhood. Do I need a haircut?"

She chuckled. "That's a matter of opinion, depending how you like your length."

"Shorter than this," he said, motioning his head. "I'll stop in next week to get acquainted and get that haircut."

"Okay. I'll look for you." Abby gave him a bright smile.

"Bye, ladies." The handsome cop walked out the door as casually as he had come in.

"Um-um," Latisha grunted. "I see sparks flying."

"Don't be silly," Abby said with a wave of her hand.

"No silliness over here. You the silly one," Latisha said.

"Go for it. I have it on good authority he's not dating anyone," Bobbi told them.

"I have a boyfriend, or sort of," Hillary said, accepting the plate from the server. "Jack's all yours."

Hillary was the only one Abby thought could be competition, but if she was interested in someone else ... Besides, it was time. She'd been divorced over a year and was feeling like she might enjoy some male companionship. Perhaps more than that.

"We'll see," was all she said.

NINE

AS PROMISED, Jack walked into the salon two days later. He didn't act awkward as some men do when surrounded by femininity and women. He wasn't in uniform. Dressed in jeans and a tee clinging to his chest, he looked every bit as yummy as he had at the deli.

"Hi, Jack." Abby glanced away from the woman's hair she was back-combing.

"Abby. Is today okay?" Jack asked.

"Sure. I'm almost done here. Just have a seat." She nodded at the chairs.

The man walked over to the seating and folded his body into the chair. Abby sprayed the woman's hair and removed the cape protecting her clothing. After she finished cashing out the client, she beckoned to Jack to come to her chair.

After he sat, Abby lowered the chair so she could reach the top of his head. "How do you like your hair done?"

"Real short on the sides, a little longer on top."

"You have nice curls on top. I hope you want to preserve them."

"You like the curls?" he asked, looking at her in the mirror.

"Well, it's not what I like. But the curls are very becoming to your face." She could see her cheeks reddening as she spoke.

"If you like them, then don't shave them off."

Abby laughed. "I wasn't planning to shave them. Just trim the curls."

"Then do it. If you think it looks good."

Well, he certainly seems interested in my preference.

After a shampoo, which made her nervous due to the close contact, she dried his hair with a towel. They returned to the chair. Abby pulled out her scissors and began shaping the man's curls to her satisfaction. She noticed he watched her as she snipped his locks. The thought of Samson and Delilah flashed through her mind.

"The shop is nice," he said. "You did good decorating."

"I didn't really do much. When was the last time you were in?"

"Never. This wasn't my patch until six months ago."

"Oh."

She shaved the back and sides of his head, realizing that all eyes were focused in her direction. Ivy practically had her tongue hanging out. Sonia frequently slid her eyes across the room. And that was just the employees. The clients were outright staring.

Sliding product between her hands, Abby demonstrated how to use it on Jack's hair. "See, just pull at places, work it in here and there. It's easy to do."

"Uh huh. I'll come in for you to do it." He grinned at her.

Abby laughed and shook her head. "You're all done," she said, wiping her hands on a towel. "You look good."

"Yeah, I agree. My hair, that is. Not the rest of me."

Abby held back a comment. *Modest, too.*

They walked to the register.

"How often should I come in?"

HAIRCUT AND HIGHLIGHTS

"Three weeks to keep it close to this. Four, if you aren't particular."

"Make an appointment for three weeks," he said, reaching in his back pocket for the wallet.

"Okay, what time?"

"Same?"

"It's open. I'll give you a card." She wrote the time and date on a business card.

He placed money on the counter to pay.

"Oh, no, this one's on me."

His blue eyes looked intently at her. "No, I have to pay."

"No, you don't. My treat for the work you do. You are appreciated."

"Oh." His eyes looked at her again, boring through. "In that case, I'm taking you to dinner for the hard work you do."

Abby was shocked by his response. "I'm not on the front line, facing down criminals."

He smiled. "Thank goodness for that. We need you here."

"Dinner?"

"Yes. How about Friday after you close? I have to make sure a pretty lady like you doesn't go hungry."

"That would be fine."

"See ya then," he said and turned to the door as he replaced his wallet.

Once he was gone, Abby turned around to see everyone staring at her. They began to applaud and call out with big smiles on their faces.

———

With a cup of coffee in hand, Abby arrived at the door to her business to find Rose lounging across the entrance on a blanket. Her face looked surprised to see her. "You said it was okay."

"Yes, I did. and it is. But you need to gather your stuff and move now, kiddo." She looked at her disheveled appearance, thinking, "*This person will never be employable.*" Rose's new haircut clung to her head and was churned around. "I have customers coming shortly."

"Got it. I'm moving." Rose quickly gathered her belongings and shoved them into the trash bag.

Abby started to say, "Your hair—"

"Yeah. Haven't washed it," she interjected.

"Oh. Don't you have somewhere to shower?"

"Yeah, when I go to the shelter. But I don't like it there."

"I see."

"Here comes the sweetheart," Rose said, looking past Abby, obviously being sarcastic.

Abby turned to see Sonia approaching. She marched to the door and stood waiting for it to be unlocked without saying a word of greeting.

"Good morning, Sonia," Abby said.

"*Si*, good morning." The woman refused to look at Rose, although she was less than two feet away.

Rose gave her the fish eye, and walked away from them.

As both women walked into the salon, Abby shook her head. Some people weren't tolerant of those less fortunate. Being Hispanic, one would think Sonia would have a better appreciation. She wasn't born here and had experienced difficulty in becoming a functioning citizen. Sonia had studied to gain the rights she now had through citizenship.

The doorbell jingled when Ivy came in. The two women automatically looked toward the door but were shocked to see her appearance. Ivy was sporting a black eye. Sonia muttered Spanish words.

"Ivy!" Abby ran over to her. "What happened?"

She pointed at her eye and saying "*Mama*", kept walking to her station.

Abby ran behind her, frantic.

"Stop! Tell me what happened."

Ivy sat in her chair and calmly relayed the story.

"Everything was fine on the ride home. Mama acted nice. She talked nice. It was all good." Ivy shrugged. "Then when we were home, she kept badgering me for money. 'You owe me rent. I can't support myself without you. You need to come back home to clean the house and make dinner for me. I can't do it all by myself.' Stuff like that."

"Then what?" asked Sonia.

"Well, after a few hours of her nagging, I told her I wasn't coming back, that I was looking for a roommate and an apartment. I said she needed to get a roommate if she needed help with expenses. That's when she slugged me." Ivy looked down at her lap, probably embarrassed.

"We need to put ice on your eye," Abby said.

"I did all that. This is the end result," she said, pointing to her eye. "I'll have to live with it."

Abby looked at Sonia for support.

"*Ay, chihuahua.* Ouch." And then she shrugged. "You have sunglasses?"

"Of course. It's Florida."

"Then wear them," Abby advised. "It's the best we can do till the color fades. No amount of coverup will camouflage *that*."

Ivy nodded in agreement and searched through her purse for sunglasses.

"Do you have appointments today?"

"Yup." She plunked the sunglasses over her eyes. "Of course, I do. I have a black eye, so I have appointments … so everyone can see my black eye."

Abby walked away, mumbling to herself. Then she turned around to face Ivy. "You'll have to explain. We have to come up with something better than you ran into a door."

"Mama took a poke at me." Sonia stated the obvious. "You'll get sympathy. Bigger tips."

Abby looked at Sonia and shook her head. "No, she can't say that. How about you fell over the dog and landed on the edge of a table?"

"Aunt Bobbi doesn't have a dog."

"No one knows that. Just pretend she has a black dog and you tripped over it during the night. Bingo, black eye."

Ivy stared at her through the dark glasses before speaking. "Okay. That works as well as anything, I guess."

Sonia left the conversation, again muttering in Spanish.

The rest of the day was spent explaining how Ivy hurt herself by falling over the dog. Whether the customers believed the story or not, supporting evidence bloomed colorfully on her upper arm and lower. Two giant bruises formed as the day went on to give authentication to her story.

By the time Abby left that day, she was relieved to have a quiet evening with Seely.

TEN

ABBY SLIPPED upstairs to change her clothes before Jack arrived. It wasn't long after she returned to the salon that he actually walked through the doors.

"Hey. You look nice, pretty lady."

She smiled from behind the register. "Thanks." Abby stuffed the bills into the bank bag, followed by the checks. "I ran upstairs to freshen up and change. I didn't want to smell like hair coloring."

"Anything but," he said, taking a whiff of her cologne from across the counter.

"I just have to secure this, and I'll be ready." She lifted the bank bag before she turned away. "Be right back."

Abby hid the bag of money and checks in her secret spot: the dirty towel hamper. Nobody with any sense of smell would dare rummage through that pile of stinky towels. She returned to the front, being sure he caught sight of her slender legs extending from a pink sundress. The matching pink sandals would naturally draw his eyes down the length of her legs.

"Do you like Cuban food?" he asked.

"I don't know that I've had it."

"Well, then, you are in for a surprise and a treat tonight." Jack opened the door for her.

"Are we walking? Or is your car one of those?" Many cars were pulled in nose-first to the curb and at an angle, a characteristic unique to Daytona and Beach Street.

"Yes. Walking. It's just around the corner." He walked with a confident air, like a man who knew who he was and where he was going in life. Abby rather liked that.

"I have to warn you, a lot of the guys from the force come here to eat. It could get noisy if they're here," Jack said.

"I won't mind."

"Good." Jack pulled the door open for her. It wasn't a large place, more intimate in ambiance. The style was masculine and dark with leather booths, stools, and chairs. A circular wooden bar rose in the center, furnishing the only obvious light. She could understand why men gathered here. It looked like the perfect place to hide after a heavy day's work or from a spouse.

"Hey, Carl," Jack called out, raising his arm to the bartender.

"Yo, Jack," the man responded from behind the bar. Several civilian males, maybe six, were scattered around the bar, nursing drinks, and talking, obviously not with law enforcement by the suits they wore.

Pointing to the left, Jack said, "We're going over here." He guided her to a booth with his hand at her back.

"Got a lady with you tonight?" asked Carl.

"Yes, and I'm not introducing her to any of you." Jack grinned at her. "She doesn't want to know the likes of you guys. Who knows? I might have to arrest you later."

"Oh, then she really is a lady," came the response.

Jack didn't continue the banter. He looked at her from across the table and smiled. "That's the owner. So, what do you think of this place?"

"Colorful. A neighborhood atmosphere. Definitely masculine."

HAIRCUT AND HIGHLIGHTS

"Good description. This is me," he said, sweeping his arm to include the room. "I come here a lot when I'm not working. I live close."

"That's safe. After drinking, you can walk home."

"True. What can I get you to drink?"

"I don't drink."

Jack looked at her with a peculiar expression. "You don't drink? I don't think I know anyone who isn't a drinker."

"Now you do."

"Seriously?"

"Seriously."

"Do you mind if I have a beer?"

"No. That's your choice."

"Do you want something?"

"A soda would be nice."

"Be right back." Jack walked to the bar.

He would just have to think she was odd not to drink. She didn't believe in imbibing. Her ex-husband had drunk enough for both of them. She didn't like what she saw after he'd been drinking, the way his mood changed and his treatment of her. She didn't need that igniting poison in her system.

"I'm back," he said, placing the beer and soda on the table. "Now, tell me why you don't drink? I'm fascinated."

Fascinated? Abby couldn't help but think that was an odd remark.

"For starters, my ex-husband was an alcoholic. That poison," she said, waving her hand at the mug of beer, "ruined him, his life, my life."

"I can understand that. What else?"

"I'm a Christian. I don't believe in drinking." She waited for his reaction.

He blinked a couple times, acting like he didn't know what to say. Then he picked up the mug and took a deep swallow. After replacing the mug on the table, he said, "At the end of a day chasing bad guys, dealing with the brass and lots of paperwork, I find it refreshing and calming to sit back and have a few."

"And I can understand that."

"So, you aren't going to judge me?"

"Of course not. I'm not your judge."

"Oh, I get it." He nodded his head. "You are certainly different from what I expected."

Abby couldn't help but smile. "You thought I was, um, maybe an airhead? A dense hairdresser? Something like that?"

"Well, not exactly. You have brains. I see that. I didn't expect the religious stuff. But that's okay." He looked at his mug awkwardly.

"Don't tell me you don't know anyone who goes to church?" she asked.

"No, I do. Definitely. My mother ... both parents, actually. Some of the guys on the force. And the wives, of course. Yeah, I know some."

"Then there's nothing to be afraid of." She said this with peace and then took a sip of her soda.

"I'm not afraid of you."

"I know. You're afraid of my beliefs."

He looked at her. "Could we change the subject? I kinda like you and I feel we got on the wrong track somehow. We can discuss all this some other time, right?"

Abby smiled at him. "Of course, we can. No problem. Tell me about your job, Jack."

The man smiled broadly, immediately jumping into what his job entailed. He chatted so long they almost didn't order dinner. Once it arrived, Abby had to agree that the food was delicious. She had ordered *arroz con pollo*, which was chicken and rice, while he chose *pulpeta*, which resembled meatloaf, except it wasn't baked but cooked on the stove. Abby sampled some of his meal and gave it a thumbs up.

HAIRCUT AND HIGHLIGHTS

"I must have been living under a rock not to have tasted Cuban food before this."

"And this place has the best I've found," he said, obviously happy she enjoyed her dinner. "We can come back here any time you want. Like I said, I come here a lot, so I never get tired of the food."

Despite a clumsy start, the date had bloomed into something promising. He wanted to go out again, and soon. Since he worked two days on and then two days off, he preferred to see her twice in a row and then take a break for two days. Abby didn't have any problem with that arrangement. On the walk home, he held her hand in his large strong one and chattered about a great movie that was playing and another one of his favorite restaurants. Since Abby hadn't been back in town long and was out of touch with the local scene, she appreciated his reviews.

Jack was a local, too. He'd never lived anywhere but Daytona Beach and had no desire to relocate. He said he was divorced with no children and didn't want any. At her age, Abby wasn't inclined in that direction, either. The relationship had all the earmarks of being successful. There was definite potential. She would just have to wait to see what happened.

As they walked and talked, crossing over the colorful bricks decorating the street, Abby spotted Rose across the four-lane road, sitting on top of a park table with her feet resting on the bench. She seemed to be observing Abby and her date. *Probably knows Jack is a cop.* Abby hoped that didn't discourage Rose from being friendly.

ELEVEN

THE NEXT MORNING, Jack came into the salon carrying two coffees. Abby noticed how Sonia greeted him with a big smile. Then his gaze fell on Ivy, black eye and all.

"What happened to your eye, kiddo?" he asked, concern washing over his face.

Ivy's eyes rounded and she didn't know what to say at first. Then, stammering, she finally choked out, "Fell over the dog."

Jack laughed. "Yeah, that's a good one, but I'm not buying it."

"Her mother did it," Abby told him.

"Do you want to press charges?" he asked, slipping into his official mode.

"Oh, no, no. I don't want to do that. No, please." Her face paled and her eyes grew bigger.

"Your mother cannot hit you. That's assault."

"It's a sticky situation, Jack. I understand why she doesn't want to. And we're all trying to help her find a roommate and an apartment," Abby interceded. "I don't think this will happen again."

He kept staring at Ivy, making her nervous. "If she touches you again, let me know."

"I will. Promise."

"Okay," he said, then turned to Abby. "Want to take a walk?"

"Sure. I have time." She slipped around the desk and out the door as Jack held it open for her. As soon as she stepped out, she smelled the ocean. How she loved that salty air!

"I had a great time last night," he said, handing a coffee to Abby.

"Me, too. And the meal was really good." She took a sip and thought how nice it was to have a man bring her coffee, prepared perfectly to her taste. He remembered.

"What's the deal with that black eye?"

"All I know is her mother gets physical with her. She's staying at her aunt's place right now. Her aunt is Bobbi, by the way. Ivy was just visiting her mother and she got mad because she wanted some of Ivy's money. Ivy said no, so she got hit. We're all trying to find her a safe place to live." Abby saw Rose across the street and waved at her.

She waved back.

"You know her?" he asked.

"Sort of. I cut her hair recently and I allow her to sleep outside my salon."

"Why?"

"Because it's the right thing to do."

"That's a matter of opinion."

"Well, my opinion, my salon." She smiled at him.

He didn't smile back. "I don't think you get the gravity of the situation." He shook his head and looped back to the salon, over the bricked street. "Those homeless will take advantage of you, steal from you, and could even harm you."

Abby gave him an indignant look. "Those homeless are people. What I've done is minor, and I felt good doing it. I'm not harmed. Nothing has been stolen. She hasn't put graffiti on my windows."

He stopped walking once they were on the sidewalk and

looked down at her. "I don't think we're going to agree on this issue. But I warned you," he said and started walking again.

"Aren't you supposed to be protecting the people? Isn't law enforcement meant to help everyone, regardless of socio-economic circumstances?"

"Yes, of course. But we learn that certain types have a tendency to do harm."

"Her 'type' hasn't done any harm."

"Yet."

"I don't think we are going to agree on this issue," she stated.

"Apparently not."

"Let's agree to disagree." She stuck out her hand.

He clasped it and said, "Agreed."

They smiled at each other over a handshake.

"All right then, I need to do some errands," he said in front of the salon. "Pick you up at six?"

"Okay. Where are we going?"

"A burger joint called Brian's Burgers. Then a movie. How's that sound?"

"Great. I'll see you at six." She smiled up at him and he swooped in for a kiss on the cheek.

"Sneak attack," she joked and turned toward her door.

"I saw that," Sonia said with a smirk as she came inside. "He kiss you in middle of sidewalk."

Abby laughed. "He's very nice. We don't agree on everything, but we don't have to. Keeps things interesting."

"*Si.*"

The ladies gathered at the deli for their Chat. Everyone ordered a drink from the cute young woman server and then looked intently at Abby.

"What?" she asked.

HAIRCUT AND HIGHLIGHTS

"Tell us about your new man," Bobbi said. "We've all seen you canoodling on the sidewalk."

"Canoodling? Well, I wouldn't call what you saw that. But, yes, we are an item," Abby told them.

"Where's he taken you?" Latisha asked.

"Our first date was at that little Cuban restaurant around the corner."

"That's where the cops hang out. I've been in there when they all come in," Hillary said, taking her drink from the server. She waited until everyone had received their beverage before continuing. "I think some of them bring their girlfriends there. The married ones, I mean."

That bit of news didn't surprise Abby. The atmosphere was perfect for that sort of thing.

"Was the food good? I've never eaten there," Bobbi asked, adding sweetener to her iced tea.

"Yes, very. I had *arroz con pollo*. Delish." She blotted her lips with a napkin.

"My husband and I will have to go there," Bobbi said.

"Where'd you go last night?" asked Hillary.

"Brian's Burgers, on the ocean. Then we went next door to get ice cream. It was fun."

"I've been there. Great burgers," Latisha nodded. "Haven't had the ice cream yet."

"That was it?" Hillary asked.

"No, we went to a movie. It was something he wanted to see and raved about. Too blood and guts for me. I like romantic comedies." Abby swirled her drink with a straw.

"Me, too. Most men like the shoot 'em up stuff. The gorier, the better. Ugh." Hillary grimaced and took a long drink from the tall glass. "I'm so thirsty with this heat."

"It's hurricane season, so it's hot. They say we're in for a hurricane," Latisha announced, all eyes focusing on her. "It's creeping toward our coast right now. Um-hm, don't want that

67

mess around here."

"I haven't been through a hurricane in years. Not a bad one, anyway." Any hurricane she'd experienced when married had been fairly mild where they were located. But now that she had a business, the thought scared Abby.

"I wonder what the homeless do during a hurricane?" she wondered aloud.

"You sure are stuck on the homeless population," Latisha said with a twist of her full lips. "Maybe they stand outside and get a good washing in the rain."

Three pairs of eyes stared at the woman. Bobbi spoke first. "I understand you don't appreciate the homeless coming around your business. I get that. But they are human beings. A hurricane could kill them if they aren't protected."

"Isn't there a shelter near the jail?" asked Abby. "Can't they go there?"

"I think they do, or maybe a church," Hillary answered.

"Whatever. You heartbreak women should invite them into your store," Latisha said flatly.

"That's a great idea," Abby said, sitting a little straighter. "I'll let Rose stay at my salon. She should be safe there."

Three pairs of eyes now looked aghast at Abby.

"Have you lost your mind?" Bobbi inquired.

"No, not at all." Abby smiled broadly. "I'll tell her in the morning."

Latisha made grunting sounds from her side of the table.

Bobbi looked over at Hillary and tried to change the subject. "How is your love life?"

Immediately her face blossomed. "At the moment, things are fine. It took some getting there, but we managed after a month's separation to think things over and decided we just couldn't stand to be apart anymore."

"You were broken up for a month, but got back together?" Abby didn't know about the situation.

"Yes. We took a break to think about things," Hillary explained.

"More like, he took a break to have himself a good time. Then you got back together when he got bored," Latisha said with a smirk.

"That's not exactly true," Hillary frowned.

"Oh, yes, it is. How many times does this make? Five break-ups? You're just too blind to see he's messing around again." Latisha turned toward Abby. "This isn't their first break-up. About every six months, he gets the itch, you know what I mean? And they break up. Then he comes back when he's done scratching, and Miss Hillary here takes him back. Every time."

"You make me sound like a moron," Hillary said, looking annoyed.

"Well, you're acting like one. I wouldn't put up with his trash for nothing," Latisha said sternly. "He plays you for a fool."

"Enough, Latisha," she said, nervously pushing hair behind her ear. "I don't want to discuss this with you."

"Fine with me."

"And moving on to other issues," Bobbi said, turning to Abby. "I think it's wonderful you're dating the cop. He's a nice guy."

"I think so, too."

"Everyone likes Jack," Latisha said, busying herself with the menu.

"Especially the ladies," Hillary remarked with a smile.

"What does that mean?" Abby asked.

"Oh, I've seen women flirt with him when he comes around. He's always charming back.

Frankly, the man doesn't hurt for companionship." She opened the menu. "He has made the rounds and gone back for seconds."

Abby let that information sink in as she walked back home. Well, of course, he dated. He was handsome, so he would be in demand. There was nothing wrong with that. As long as he wasn't seeing other women while he was dating her. He hadn't given any indication of having interest in other women. She couldn't imagine how he would find time with his schedule. She put that thought out of her head and focused on her surroundings.

What a delight to live and work on a street so artistically decorated. Where else could she find aqua, wrought-iron archways? And the palm trees interspersed along both sides of the street simply screamed Florida. Abby was so grateful to have returned to Daytona.

TWELVE

FURRY PAWS WALKED over Abby's face, waking her from a sound sleep. "Murph, thwiff," she sputtered, wiping fur from her mouth. "You little imp."

The kitten winked two blue eyes at her in response.

"Okay, I'm getting up," she said, rising from under the covers with a slam of bare feet on the floor. "But first things first."

Abby went into the bathroom before heading to the kitchen to make coffee and breakfast for Seely. The furball came scampering into the kitchen, all white and pretty. A tinge of color was growing at the tip of her tail and rimmed the edge of her ears. So far, no coloring was showing on her face.

"Mama's pretty girl. Yes, here's your breakfast," she told the kitten as she sat the plate on the floor. She couldn't help but give her a loving stroke as the kitten lapped up the food. Then Abby got ready for work.

When she arrived at her salon, Rose was packing up her sleeping quarters. "Rose? Here's some coffee," she said, sticking her arm out toward the woman.

Rose reached for the coffee with a smile on her face. "Thanks. Nice of you."

"Listen, Rose, there's a hurricane predicted to be coming up the coast. No doubt we'll at least get heavy storms and wind, even if it veers off a bit. I can let you stay inside the salon."

Rose's eyes widened considerably. "Really? You would do that?"

"Sure, I would."

The woman lowered her head, then raised it, looking into Abby's eyes. "Why would you do that? I could burn the place down."

Abby laughed. "I don't believe that for an instant. Rose, I'm just trying to help you. You are welcome to stay inside, where it's safe."

Through moist eyes, Rose said, "Thank you. No one has done anything for me for a long time. No one cares about me."

"*I* care, Rose." Abby's gaze expressed her sincerity. "I really want to help you."

Rose blinked her eyes. "Okay. I'd like to stay here."

"I don't have a bed for you, but you can stretch out on the couch. There's a bathroom in the back, and plenty of towels if you want to clean up."

"That sounds great. Better than a normal night, let alone during a hurricane," she said with a grin.

"Then it's settled. At the end of the day, I'll get you inside. If you want to leave, just pull the door shut behind you, okay?"

"Yes, okay." She took a sip of her coffee, her eyes smiling over the edge of the cup.

―――

Abby hesitated to mention her arrangement with Rose to anyone for fear Sonia would throw a conniption fit. Why did she have to know anyway? This was her business, and she could do as she pleased. Where was the harm? There wasn't anything worth stealing unless Rose wanted to take a bottle of hair dye.

HAIRCUT AND HIGHLIGHTS

Really? And as for damage, Abby couldn't imagine Rose would be destructive. What would be the point of that?

Sonia was busy teasing a client's hair when Ivy walked from the back, wearing a big smile.

"What brings such a pretty smile to your face today?" asked Abby as she put her coffee
on her station and plopped her purse on the chair.

"I have a new place to stay," she answered, clasping her hands in front, and doing a little jump.

"Really? That's wonderful. Walk with me and tell me about it." She picked up her purse and headed to the backroom.

"Well, you wouldn't believe ... but Aunt Bobbi saved the day. A regular customer of hers came into the shop and happened to mention having a vacant room. Something about her grandson having moved out for college. So, Aunt Bobbi asked her if she had plans to rent the room."

"And she did?"

"Yes. Only $35 a week, and I have kitchen privileges."

"That sounds pretty cheap."

"I can easily do that in one day from my tips," she said, shoving her hands into the pockets of her black smock. "She's a sweet old lady. The house is probably a hundred years old and has lots of rooms. My room is real cute, with a four-poster bed and a darling dresser."

"Where's it located?"

"Just one block behind us, on Palmetto. I can walk to work."

"It sounds perfect for you, Ivy," Abby smiled.

"It is. Now Aunt Bobbi can get her spare bedroom back, and not have me under foot."

"I'm sure you weren't under foot. She loves you."

"Well, it's time I had my own place and not have to duck flying fists." Ivy rolled her eyes.

"What's the woman's name?"

"You know her. It's Mrs. York."

Of course, she knew Mrs. York. She was her first client here. "Oh, yes. She is a nice lady." Abby embraced Ivy. "Good job, kiddo. Things are turning around for you."

Ivy grinned. "I'll say."

"I wonder … how do you feel about changing your hair color?" Abby asked as she fingered her curly strands.

"My red hair? Why? It's my signature," Ivy said, flustered.

"Honey, your signature doesn't become you. It's too bright, not a believable color."

"Oh." Ivy looked disappointed. "I like it."

"But it doesn't like you. If we added brown, we could make you chestnut or auburn. You'd still have some reddish highlights, but they would be more natural." Abby paused and regarded her intently. "What do you think?"

"I think you know best. You have the experience; I don't."

"You *want* me to do it?"

"Yes. Do it," she replied firmly.

"Okay! A total makeover coming up!" Abby went to the supply room for the color. When she returned, she had something soapy in a cup.

"Come over to the shampoo bowl. I'm doing a soap cap on you to remove some of your color."

Ivy followed Abby to the shampoo bowls.

Abby applied a mix of bleach and shampoo to Ivy's hair, then covered it with a clear cap. "Sit there, and I'll come back when you're done."

When Abby returned, she examined Ivy's hair. "Perfect." Then she shampooed Ivy and brought her back to the chair where she used the blow dryer.

Once the hair was dry, she applied the new hair color. They waited the recommended time and when the timer chimed, she washed out the color. After Abby finished styling Ivy's hair, she turned the young woman around to face the mirror.

Ivy's mouth fell open at her reflection. "I can't believe it," she said breathlessly.

"Next is the makeup," Abby informed her. "I don't think you need much, though. Some mascara will bring out your long lashes. Blush, of course. Then lipstick. Or do you prefer gloss?"

"I don't know. I don't wear either."

"Well, you do now. Wear it every day." Abby applied the mascara artfully, then spun pink powder over Ivy's cheeks. "Customers expect you to wear makeup."

"Whatever you say," Ivy said between dabs of a rose lipstick applied to her mouth.

"Now, look at yourself," Abby instructed, standing behind Ivy. "You're so pretty."

Ivy looked at herself. The face that stared back resembled a young woman more than a girl. Her blue eyes seemed to jump out, and her lips were well shaped. "I don't know if I'd agree I'm pretty, but I look a lot better."

Abby smiled. "You are now auburn, and you look *wonderful*."

Sonia, having been at a dentist appointment, had missed the transformation. When she walked into the salon five minutes later, she exclaimed, "*Ay caramba*, she's a goddess!"

Abby and Ivy laughed.

THIRTEEN

THE WIND HAD PICKED up from blowing as a pleasant breeze, uncharacteristic for the summer months, to gusting seventy-five miles an hour. The rain was pelting down, stinging like biting insects when it contacted the skin. People in Daytona Beach were seeking cover or hiding in their homes, bracing for the hurricane's onslaught. Some had probably left the coast in an attempt to avoid the storm, while others had decided to tough it out. However, the prediction now was that the city would receive a glancing blow from Hurricane Ethel. Mandatory evacuation was not in affect.

The sea roared its might and sent waves that every surfer dreamed about onto the sands of Daytona Beach. Since the fear of flooding was always present, even on the mainland, Abby had stuck towels at the entrance to her salon. If this had been a bad hurricane, as initially predicted, she would have obtained sandbags for the outside. Jack had said she would probably be okay, so she didn't make that effort. However, she did also place numerous towels at the door leading upstairs to the apartments. It couldn't hurt.

Rose was settled into the salon, safe and sound. If there was

HAIRCUT AND HIGHLIGHTS

a problem, she could use the phone there to call Abby, who would be upstairs. However, most homeless were given phones for their protection. Whether she had one or not, Abby had not asked.

So far, Abby was seeing very heavy rain from her window, and strong winds, but not dangerous hurricane-force winds, for which she was grateful. She noticed that few cars were on the bridge, which rose high to meet the rain. As she looked across Beach Street, she saw the expensive yachts anchored to the dock, bobbing in the Halifax River as if they were toys in a child's bathtub. That's when she heard a knock at her door.

"Anyone there?" a male voiced asked.

"Coming," she said as she walked over. When she opened her door, there stood a very handsome blonde man, complete with broad shoulders, a deep chest, and overall muscles. He was dressed in a tee with suspenders looped over his shoulders, and roomy pants below.

"I'm your neighbor," he said, pointing to the back apartment. "Mark Hudson. I was checking to see if you were all right or needed some help."

Abby was left almost speechless after seeing him. He was quite the hunk and seemed caring. She almost forgot about the hurricane.

"Oh, hi, yes, I am okay. I was watching the hurricane. Or is it a storm?" she asked.

The man grinned. "It appears to have diminished but will probably continue at this level for hours. Or we may just get heavy rain. I don't think we're in for a rough time this go round."

"I am so relieved to hear that," she smiled. "I have the hair salon just below, so I am rather invested in the outcome."

"I understand. I'm a fireman, stationed just over there, next to the marina. So far, we're good," he explained. "But I wanted to make sure you were okay."

"Yes, I'm fine." She smiled into his face, noting the short, clean-cut hair. "I'm Abby Bugsly. It was very nice of you to check on me."

"No problem." He gave her a bright smile, complete with even, white teeth. "If something happens, just let me know. I'll be over there."

"I will."

And he was gone.

Abby shut the door, then leaned against it, muttering, "Wow, this is my neighbor? What a heart throb! He should be in one of those firemen calendars." His physique was certainly every bit as excellent as the ones she had viewed in those calendars. And he was her neighbor? *Lucky me.*

Abby moved to a chair near the window so she could watch the storm. And think about her neighbor. Seely joined her, purring as she was petted.

Rose was stretched out on the couch, feeling dry, safe, and content. She rolled to one side, staring out at the storm. The rain lashed the windows with gusto. The wind propelled the rain with intense bursts, but not strong enough to cause damage to the windows. A wall of glass protected her from the elements, unlike most nights. She didn't know why Abby had taken a shine to her. What possessed this nice woman to care if she was safe? No one else did. For Abby to offer her place of business so she had safety from the storm was incredibly kind. It gave Rose pause.

She watched a streak of lightning rip across the sky, briefly brightening the salon interior. She could have been on the receiving end of that bolt. Permanently having her life snuffed out in a flash. No more. Who would miss her if that had happened? No one she could think of. Everyone who had meant

HAIRCUT AND HIGHLIGHTS

anything to her was either dead or long gone from her world. Unlike many homeless, she wasn't a mental case. No drugs were necessary to keep her sane, although some might think she was insane to live like this. But Rose knew she was of sound mind. It was life that had sent her into this homeless world, not an unbalanced mind. And people. Yes, people had played a large part in her situation.

It had started with abusive parents—in particular, her father. She had to flee; there had been no choice at the time. But at that age, she was feisty, stubborn, and determined to have a better life. And she succeeded for a while. Years. Then everything crashed around her. First, it was her job. Her new boss was a Type A personality, demanding like a drill sergeant. He was intimidating and critical, making her feel she could never please him. One day, she stood up for herself and that proved to be fatal. She was fired for insubordination.

Then she was evicted from her apartment because she couldn't find a job due to being fired. But she still had her car. The Malibu became her bedroom, living area, and sometimes her kitchen. How she'd loved that car. It had kept her dry and safe for two years—until it was towed for being in a no parking zone. Stupid. Why she had done that, she didn't know. Just plain stupid. And then, she was on the street.

Rose got up from the couch to use the restroom. When she finished, she looked at herself in the mirror. Her brown hair was flat to her head. The least she could have done was wash her hair once in a while after Abby was so kind to cut it for her. Where had her pride gone? She used to be so particular about her appearance. Rose had worn makeup, dressed nicely. And she'd loved fragrance, having several scents on her dresser. What had happened to that woman? Where had she gone? Was that person still living inside her, buried deep? Or had that woman disintegrated into oblivion?

She walked out of the restroom, feeling totally disgusted

with herself. Rose had been so strong, rising above every circumstance thrown at her. She had always landed on her feet. *Always.* So what if people didn't want to hire her? She'd found a better job anyway. But this last bad break had devastated her, torn up her confidence like a sheet of paper. Rose had seen no way out when the domino effect came at her. Everything grew worse, until the day she was on the street, homeless.

Rose lay on the couch again, tears moistening her cheeks. She hadn't cried in a very long time. But previously, she hadn't allowed thoughts of the past to invade. That was dangerous. She was already down in a pit. There was nowhere lower. Or was there? That thought chilled her to the bone. Rose cried herself to sleep.

FOURTEEN

ROSE SLEPT HARD ONCE she fell asleep.

Abby woke her as she entered the salon in the morning, holding two coffee cups in her hands. "Rose? You okay?" she asked as the woman stirred on the couch.

"Um, yeah." Rose yawned loudly as she sat up. She wiped her eyes and looked at Abby.

"Coffee?" she asked, placing a cup on the table nearby.

"Yes, wonderful. Thank you." She reached for the brew.

"Did you sleep all right?" Abby asked, sitting across from the woman.

"Very sound. The couch is comfy," she replied with a smile.

"Good. I was afraid the storm would keep you awake."

"I got used to it." Rose sipped her coffee and smiled. "I've slept in worse conditions."

"I guess you have. My doorstep can't be that great," Abby said ruefully.

"But it's safe. And kind of you to offer it."

Abby looked at her kindly. "Rose ... *why?*"

Two eyes looked at Abby over the cup. She responded with one word. "Life."

"Okay. We've all had bad breaks. But we can turn things around if we make the effort," Abby stated, trying to understand this woman across from her.

Rose chuckled. "I made the effort, but all the stars were against me, I guess. Nothing ever turned around for me. I just kept sinking lower. So, here I am."

Abby's heart broke hearing the woman's words. "Rose, I'll help you. Look at me, Rose." Abby held the woman's gaze. "I will help you get on your feet again. I promise. You just have to let me."

Rose eyed her cautiously in return.

"I really will. You may not believe me, but I will help you. People may have let you down, but I won't, Rose. I'm not like that." Abby's face swam with sincerity as she continued to stare into Rose's face. "Please, Rose."

The woman looked down at her hands, then held them up. "Look at my hands, my nails. They're dirty. I'm dirty. I probably made this couch filthy with my grime."

"So? Everything can be washed clean, especially you." Abby wasn't giving up.

Rose let her body fall back into the pillows. It was her turn to ask, "Why?"

"Because you're worth it. You are God's daughter, a special soul," Abby answered.

"Yeah, I've heard stuff like that at the church when they feed us. We're all children of God. He loves me unconditionally. I get it." She slid lower into the couch.

"But you're not impressed?"

"If I'm so special, why is He letting me live like this? Why doesn't He help me?"

"Have you asked?"

Rose's eyes jumped to Abby's face in surprise. "No," she said softly.

"Maybe you want to start there."

HAIRCUT AND HIGHLIGHTS

Rose sat silently on the couch, sipping coffee. Abby slipped away to open the salon, letting the woman think quietly.

Ten minutes later, Rose walked over to the desk, dragging her bag. "I better head out. You'll have customers coming soon. And Sergeant Pardon won't like me being here."

"You know him?" Abby asked.

"We all know him, and he knows every one of us, too," she replied. "He makes a point of keeping tabs on us. He'll find out I stayed here. He knows I sleep outside your salon."

"He never mentioned knowing you." Abby wondered why he hadn't mentioned knowing Rose when they were discussing—or disagreeing—about the homeless.

"Well, he does."

"Don't worry about what he thinks. Think about what I said, Rose."

"I will." She turned toward the door, then looked back before she left. "I really *will* think about it." She flashed a smile, then left.

Abby stood with her hands in the register, thinking about what had happened. Had she said the right words? Would Rose think about her offer? Would she ask God for help? She shook her head because she had no answers. Silently, she said a prayer for Rose. As she finished, Sonia walked in.

"*Ay caramba*, such ugly weather!" The woman cast her eyes on Abby. "But no damage?"

"No, I can't find any damage to the place, fortunately," she answered, closing the register.

"Ooh, I so scared last night. I shake in the bed," she said as she sashayed across the salon. "My honey couldn't come be with me."

"Which one? Jose?"

"Ah, no. He gone. Manuel. He special," she answered with a big grin on her face.

Abby remembered Sonia saying Jose was special, too. Maybe they were all special to her in some way. While they lasted.

Ivy came in the door, breathless. "I had to run to get here on time. Tree limbs and branches are down all over the place. It's a mess out there."

"Was there any damage to Mrs. York's house?" Abby asked.

"No, but a tree fell in the backyard. An old oak. Sad." Ivy threw her backpack under her station. "I'm getting some coffee. Anyone want some?"

Abby and Sonia both said no to the offer.

"Back in a flash," she said as she went out the door.

"I'm going to walk down to Dress 4 Success. Are you okay while I'm gone?" Abby asked.

"*Si.* I just sit here," Sonia replied, sitting in her chair, filing her nails.

Abby walked past Memories, waving at Bobbi, then Cat's Meow, but she didn't see Latisha inside. *Must be in the back.* She pulled open the door to Hillary's shop, looking around.

"I'm back here," Hillary called.

Abby walked toward a side row of pants, where Hillary was clipping clothes to hangers. "Hey. How are you?"

"I'm good. Just got some new things in, so I'm putting them out." Hillary hung up two articles on the display rack. "What's up?"

"Remember your offer to donate some clothes to Rose? I'd like to take you up on that," Abby said and waited for a response.

"Sure. I can do that. Does she have a job interview?" she asked, continuing to clip more clothes to hangers.

"Not yet, but I have hopes. She stayed inside the salon last night and we had a talk this morning. I told her I'd help her get on her feet. She'll need clothes to do that."

"She sure will."

"Rose is thinking about my offer, and I really believe she will do it. She seems a little different since last night."

"Maybe staying where it's safe and dry had an impact. Or your offer to allow her to stay there impressed her enough to trust you." Hillary shrugged as she looked at Abby.

"It's hard to say, but she was different. She talked pretty openly with me, made me feel she's on the brink of a change … like something happened last night."

"Do you want to bring Rose in? She should try on the clothes, see what she likes, and if they fit,"

Abby nodded. "I think that would be best. Maybe a little 'girl time' would bring back memories. Sort of get her moving in the right direction."

"You know my hours, so bring her by any time. I suggest she have a bath before she comes."

Hillary was making a reasonable request. Perhaps she would have Rose shower in her own apartment? "I'll make sure she's clean before we come," Abby said, reaching her arms out to Hillary. "Thank you."

"You're most welcome," Hillary said, returning the hug.

Abby walked back to her salon, feeling like things were coming together with Rose. How she wanted to help this woman get on the right path. Rose had value. With a little assistance, she could get on her feet again. Maybe Mrs. York would rent a room to Rose? That would be a wholesome environment for her. And not expensive. Her heart sang over the prospects for Rose as she returned to her salon.

FIFTEEN

SEELY WAS BEING A TOTAL BRAT. Not only had she stomped all over Abby's face to wake her up, she'd meowed in the process. When Seely wanted something, she bellowed loudly, and sometimes directly into Abby's ear.

"*What?*" Abby sat up in bed, glaring at the kitten beside her. Seely was growing darker on her ears and tail, a nice brown contrast to the cream body. "You can't be *that* hungry."

"Purp."

"I guess that was a yes." She swung her legs over the edge of the bed and made her way to the bathroom. Once that task was completed, she went into the kitchen to make coffee and breakfast for the kitten. While Seely ate and the coffee perked, Abby got ready for her day.

Finally ready to leave, she took an extra coffee with her to give to Rose. With two cups of coffee in hand, she exited the entrance to the upstairs apartments. She turned, as usual, to the left toward her shop, but saw what she thought was a foot sticking beyond the beginning of the store front. Maybe Rose was still sleeping? She drew closer and saw that it was a lone shoe lying on its side. Rose was not there, nor was any other homeless person.

But a red substance was spread all over the cement and sprinkled on the windows above. Was this blood? Did the shoe belong to Rose? Then the worst thought came crashing in: was this Rose's blood?

Abby attempted to stifle a scream, clasping a hand over her mouth, then turned toward the street so she didn't see what she knew had to be blood. Setting the coffees on the sidewalk, she fumbled with her purse, pulling out her cell phone and dialing 911. When the dispatcher came on the line, she gave a brief account of what she found, and answered questions.

"Yes, it looks like blood to me. And it's everywhere, up the windows, all around the

entrance to my salon."

The dispatcher asked more questions.

"No, I don't see anyone around." Abby glanced down Beach Street, up Volusia Avenue, and saw nothing.

The dispatcher said the police were on the way; it should be momentary before they arrived.

"Yes, I'll stay on the line."

It wasn't long before she heard sirens screaming. One police car came to an abrupt halt at the corner of Volusia Avenue, while another came from the south, crossed Beach Street, and parked at the corner, the noses of their two vehicles almost meeting. Two uniformed men jumped out of the squad car on Volusia, two exited on Beach, leaving their vehicles idling.

"Are you hurt?" one officer asked.

"No, I'm fine. But someone must have been hurt." Abby pointed behind, with her thumb at the blood three feet away.

While the first officer asked questions, the others blocked pedestrians from coming near the crime scene. Abby heard more sirens screaming.

"And who are you?" asked the officer.

"I'm Abby Bugsly. I own this shop."

"What can you tell me about this blood?"

"Not much. It was here when I came to work. But I do let a homeless woman sleep here," she replied. "This could be her blood. And then there's the shoe." She gestured.

"Do you know the name of the homeless woman, maybe someone who would do this to her?" he asked.

"Her name is Rose Tumbler. I have no idea who would do this to her, or if it's even her blood," she said, turning away her face.

Ivy and Sonia arrived for work engaged in animated conversation, then stopped in place, gasping at the sight before them.

The officer threw up his hands. "Ladies, step back, please. Move on. We can't block the sidewalk."

"These are my employees," Abby advised him.

"You should send them home. Your salon isn't opening today," he said.

An official vehicle pulled up on the curb. Jack stepped out. "Holy cow, what do we have here?"

"Blood, sir." He pointed at Abby. "She's the owner of the shop."

"I know. Abby? What's going on?" He looked at her with surprise and compassion.

"I-I just came and, well, there w-was all this blood e-everywhere," Abby stammered. "And ... the shoe."

"Ladies, come over here, away from the scene." Jack led them closer to Bobbi's storefront.

Ivy looked petrified and was silent. Sonia was chattering in Spanish at the speed of a clapping castanets. Abby didn't have words to connect into a sentence, so she followed silently.

"Okay, I know this is difficult, but I'm asking you to be calm. Please stay quiet and out of the way while we do the investigation. I need to step over here, to the scene." Jack moved toward the other men and engaged them to find out what had occurred.

HAIRCUT AND HIGHLIGHTS

Abby looked sadly at the two other women, unsure what to say or do. "I think you should go home. We can't work here today, not with blood splattered across the entrance. You'll have to call your clients and tell them."

Sonia whipped out her cell and began punching numbers, speaking in Spanish once she had someone on the line.

"At some point, I'll post a sign to let people know we aren't open," Abby said. "Go home, Ivy. We'll talk later." Abby gave her a halfhearted smile.

The girl nodded and turned away to walk home to her apartment.

Jack returned. "This will take time. You don't need to stay. I can interview you later."

"Can we put a notice on the door that we're closed due to, well, an unfortunate incident?" She looked up into his face as she spoke, eyes wide.

"Sure, of course. I'll get some paper from the car and write it out for you."

"Thank you."

"I'll be in touch."

"Sarge," one of the men yelled.

"I've got to go." He turned toward his duty.

Abby opened the downstairs door beside the salon and walked up two flights. Each step felt like her feet had cement blocks attached. Finally winding around the corner of the banister, she was short of breath. *Glad I'm not any older.*

When she unlocked her door, the kitten came scampering to her. She let out a loud meow of greeting.

"Hello, you. How was your morning? ... Oh, really? That dull. Well, I've got a story for you."

She threw her purse on the couch, then sat beside it. Seely climbed over the fabric like a pro till she reached her owner. Abby allowed her head to fall back and sighed. That was when she saw the vase on the kitchen counter lying on its side, water spilled onto the surface and one lone rose, wilting.

"Did you do that? Of course, you did. Such a brat."

Abby rose to mop up the water and rescue the flower. When she went to throw the paper towel in the trash, she found the container upturned and the contents strewn around. "Coffee grounds," she sighed. "Nice."

She looked at the kitten enthusiastically rubbing her ankles. "What am I going to do with you? If you weren't such a good conversationalist, I'd have to get rid of you." Of course, she would never do that.

Abby finished cleaning up the mess just as she heard a knock on the door. She anticipated it was Jack, which it was.

"I need to get your statement," he said as he entered. "Oh, nice apartment." He glanced around, nodding his approval. "How about we sit at that counter?" he suggested, walking toward it.

Abby followed behind.

Jack had papers in his hands, which he organized, and then began to write on. "I know your name, have the address ... okay, tell me what happened."

Abby gave him all the details of her discovery of the blood on her doorstep and windows.

"What was the time?"

"It must have been eight-thirty. That's when I usually arrive. I like to get there ahead of the other ladies," she said.

"Was anyone else standing around?" he asked, looking at the paper he was writing on.

"I didn't see anyone. Not even across the street."

Jack continued to write as she spoke. He opened his mouth to ask another question and instead let out a yell. Looking at his leg, he saw a white kitten heading north, her claws providing the transportation. Then he swore. "Get that thing off me!"

HAIRCUT AND HIGHLIGHTS

Seely had made it to his bent knee, so she stopped, looking into the man's face. Her purr of approval was loud.

"Ooh Seely, come here," Abby coaxed.

"When did you get a cat?"

"Pretty soon after I moved in here. And she's a kitten, with needle-like claws, as you've noticed." Abby held the kitten in her lap, stroking it.

Jack glowered at the tiny feline. "I'm not too thrilled with cats."

"That's too bad," she smiled. "You don't know what you're missing."

"Yeah, I do. Torn up legs."

Abby giggled.

"Where were we?"

"About the time you arrived on the scene," she replied.

"What did I miss before that?"

"Nothing else I can think of. The officer had just asked us to move," she said, continuing to stroke Seely.

"Do you have any idea where the blood could have originated from?" Jack stared intently into her face.

"I have absolutely no clue. I am guessing it could belong to Rose Tumbler, my homeless lady, but I only say that because I allow her to sleep at the entrance to my store." The kitten was getting antsy in her lap, so it sprang over to Jack's lap.

"Uh, you're back," he said, regarding the furry creature. "I didn't invite you."

The kitten kept staring at Jack's face, then reached a tiny paw to tap his chin as he bent closer.

"Now, you have to admit she's cute."

Jack straightened. "No, I don't."

Seely decided to leap onto the counter, away from Jack's lap. When she landed, her little paws skewed all the papers, so some fell to the floor. Again, Jack swore.

"I'll get the papers." Abby rose from the stool.

"Why don't you get that monster out of here? Lock her up somewhere," he suggested gruffly.

After Abby gathered the papers and replaced them on the counter, she picked up Seely, and put her in the bathroom behind a closed door.

"Satisfied?" she asked upon return.

"Yes. Where were we before the white bomber scattered everything?"

"I don't know."

"Have you seen this Rose woman with anyone?" he asked.

"Not lately. I saw her with a homeless guy once, sitting on the park bench. I don't know if she has friends. But you should know. She told me you know her," Abby said.

"Yeah, I know everyone. That's my job. The guy you saw was probably her boyfriend, Sam. Okay, so we've established the blood might belong to Rose Tumbler," he said in summation. "No idea who would want to harm her, if that is her blood, and she's homeless. That's not much to go on."

"No, it's not." Abby gave him a discouraged look. "Maybe her boyfriend hurt her?"

"A possibility. We'll do forensics on the evidence we gathered from the crime scene. That may give us some leads. I know the boyfriend's name, so we'll try to run him down. But it could be tough. If they don't want to be found, they're really good at hiding. We need to know if that's her blood."

"I understand. And what about all that blood?" she asked, concerned over the gross mess at her storefront.

"A hazmat crew will clean it up. Should be today. Doesn't look good to have a storefront with blood all over it. Scares people." He gathered his papers.

"And it's bad for business."

Jack looked kindly at Abby. "Don't worry, kiddo. Everything will be fine."

"I sure hope you're right."

SIXTEEN

THE LADIES HAD GATHERED for the Chat again. Naturally, their conversation centered around the bloody scene in front of Goldilocks, right on their street.

"I didn't know anything was going on at your place until I heard the sirens. I came in my shop through the back door, so I never saw the blood before all the ruckus began," Bobbi stated. "Then, when I stuck my head out to see what was going on, I was horrified."

"I couldn't see the blood from my place," Hillary said. "I'm grateful for that. All I saw was the patrol cars, and then a bunch of cops running around."

"I went to the curb so I could get a good look," Latisha told them, which caused everyone to stare in disbelief. "Hey, it's not the first blood I've seen! I grew up in the south side of Chicago. We had regular stabbings."

"I've never seen a stabbing, and I don't want to ever see that much blood again," Abby murmured.

"You poor thing," Hillary said, placing one hand on her arm. "Such an experience to live through."

"Maybe they came for you, Abby, and got your homeless lady instead?" suggested Latisha. "Do you know some hoods?"

"Latisha! That's uncalled for," Bobbie said sternly, giving the woman a deep frown.

"Well, it could be true. Mistaken identity. Somebody could think she has money 'cause she owns a shop. You have to admit, that's logical," Latisha said, leaning back in her chair and stirring her coffee.

Bobbi rolled her eyes. "It's just as logical that the homeless woman's boyfriend tried to kill her. He knew where she'd be sleeping."

"Jack did say she had a boyfriend," Abby noted.

"I think this somehow involves romance. A lover scorned," suggested Hillary.

"All you think about is romance," Latisha said, sliding her brown eyes over to Hillary. "What kind of romance do you think homeless people have?"

"I don't know. It's not like I associate with the homeless," Hillary said, bringing her cup to her lips and taking a quick sip. "Don't they form bonds? You know, like they protect each other?"

"Anything is possible," Abby said. "It could be my fault. Maybe one dude got jealous because a new one was interested after she looked better with her new haircut."

"Don't blame yourself, Abby." Bobbi crossed her arms in front of her chest. "I don't know much about the homeless, but your bit of kindness didn't get her attacked. There's more to this story than we know. *And* we don't know for sure if that's her blood. She could have spent the night somewhere else."

"And it could be she was in the wrong place at the wrong time," Latisha added. "For all we know, she might have had drugs on her, or money. Some other homeless person tried to kill her for what she had. Just that simple. Happens all the time in Chicago."

HAIRCUT AND HIGHLIGHTS

"We're not in Chicago. People don't get knifed to death on Beach Street. It just doesn't happen," Hillary declared, returning the cup to the saucer. "At least, I've never heard of such."

"Neither have I," said Bobbi, uncrossing her arms.

"Or me, but I haven't been here as long as you all," Abby said.

"We can beat this rug to death, but it isn't going to solve who killed Rose," Latisha stated flatly. "Let the police figure it out."

"If she was the one killed. *If.* It could be someone else. Let's change the subject," Abby suggested.

"How's your love life, Hillary?" asked Bobbi.

The pretty blonde immediately blushed with her response. "Wonderful! He's being so attentive. He took me out to dinner twice in one week, and he says he can't stand being away from me more than a couple hours."

"That's long enough to—"

Latisha was cut off by Bobbi's stern look. "Never mind."

"Yes, never mind your negative thoughts. This time, I think it's for real," said Hillary. "I think he's learned his lesson. He's back to stay. Who knows? We could get engaged."

Latisha harrumphed from her chair.

"That's wonderful, Hillary," Bobbi said, trying to soothe the situation. "I hope it all works out just the way you want it."

"Thank you, Bobbi. You are a true friend." Hillary smiled to herself, happiness written all over her face.

Abby left the deli, taking a slow walk back to her apartment, enjoying the scenery. The yachts looked so peaceful swaying on the water where they were docked. She wondered if she'd ever be in a position to afford such luxury. Up ahead, she was surprised to see a large man hanging around, near the door to her salon.

He was dirty, with gnarly hair pointed in every direction, and torn clothes. His beard was unkempt, and Abby could only imagine how he smelled. She hadn't noticed him hanging around before. What bothered her most was his interest in the salon. He was peering inside, then walked to the door leading upstairs to the apartments. He didn't enter, much to her relief. Finally, he moved on. *Who is this character?*

SEVENTEEN

THE SERVER at the deli brought their lunch to the table in the corner where they hoped to have privacy. Abby eyed her chicken Caesar salad approvingly. Jack lifted the top of the bun on his burger to add catsup. Satisfied he had the perfect amount, he closed the burger and took a big, juicy bite. His lips glistened from the juice and catsup as he looked across the table at Abby.

"Um, you have a little, uh, stuff," she said, pointing at her own lips.

"Sorry." He wiped away the evidence with a napkin.

"Are you opposed to saying grace?"

"Uh, no. Why?" He stopped the burger midway to his mouth.

"Because you never suggest saying grace before we eat. At least, you haven't so far."

"I guess it's not a habit of mine."

"Then you don't object to saying grace?"

"No, not at all," he said, looking like he wasn't sure how to answer.

"Then you wouldn't mind if *I* said grace?" she asked. Abby always said grace. It was how she'd been brought up.

"No, of course not. Go right ahead." Jack sat back in his chair and waited.

Abby said a simple prayer of grace, followed by "amen".

Jack leaned forward to his burger and resumed eating.

"Where are you in the investigation?" she asked as she sliced her chicken.

"Forensics were scarce, since there wasn't a weapon left at the scene. Some hair was found. Mainly, the evidence was blood, two different samples. And the shoe."

"Does the shoe belong to Rose?"

"That's hard to say without asking her. We have to find her to do that," he replied. "But the shoe didn't have any blood on it. Since it's a mary-jane style, blood would have gone inside, too."

Abby's eyes narrowed. "What about the blood? What did DNA turn up?"

"And then there's that," Jack nodded. He took a big bite of his burger, visibly enjoying the taste. "See, the DNA results point to a male on both the samples, so it's not Rose who was attacked. I know you don't want to hear this, but your friend Rose could be the one who did the stabbing. If, in fact, she was even involved. You have to consider she may not have been anywhere near."

"I see." She slipped lettuce between her lips, pausing before she spoke, holding her fork in midair. "Not to change the subject, but doesn't it bother you to eat meat with red catsup when talking about a bloody crime scene?"

He stopped eating to respond. "No. This isn't my first rodeo. I've seen plenty of bloody crime scenes. I'm conditioned to it."

"Oh." She dropped her eyes to the salad again, glad this was what she was eating. Nothing was red. "What do you do now?"

"Besides look for Rose and her boyfriend, ask a lot of questions," he said with a smile. "Every homeless person we run into, we'll ask a slew of questions, such as, where's Rose? Someone knows something, but they sure aren't going to hunt us down to tell us anything."

"That's too bad. I wish there was something I could do to help," Abby said, dabbing at her lips with her napkin. "I can look to see if she's sleeping at my storefront."

"It's best you stay out of it and let us handle the case."

"Yes, Sgt. Pardon," she said with a smirk and an animated salute.

"Okay, wise guy," Jack said, grinning. "As they say in the movies: let the professionals handle it."

"Roger." She resumed eating.

I'll look for her tonight. Abby wanted to know if Rose was injured or needed her help and, most importantly, was she still alive? She hadn't seen Rose in a couple of days, and she was more than a little concerned.

———

Abby didn't know when Rose was prone to arrive for sleep. For all she knew, the woman could come around at three in the morning. Not knowing what she did during the day, let alone at night, she imagined Rose could be panhandling outside the bars until the wee hours, or doing something illegal. She set the alarm for three in an attempt to locate her downstairs if she returned for sleep. *Maybe this is crazy?*

When the alarm let out a rude clanging noise, she got up, left her front door ajar, and made her way down the staircase on her tiptoes so as not to wake her neighbors. She never saw anyone on the street going upstairs or in the hallways of the building, so she didn't know how many neighbors she had. Occasionally, she heard people talking on the stairs, or movement overhead, so she knew someone lived there besides the fireman.

She pushed open the front door, looking in both directions before she ventured to the sidewalk. Seeing no one, she let the door close softly behind. When she came to the front of her salon, she found it vacant. No homeless person was there. She returned immediately to the front door, unlocking it, and entering. Abby climbed the stairs, hearing music on her floor coming from the apartment behind. *Mark must be a night owl or has an early shift.*

Abby pushed open her door, walked inside, and turned the deadbolt. That was enough investigating. There was still time for more sleep. She snuggled back in bed thinking, "I didn't find Rose, but at least I didn't find any more blood."

Ruby Moskowitz bustled into the salon early the next morning, looking a bit flustered. "Hot, bloody hot out there." Her red coif was askew, adding to the impression she was making on everyone. She was a string-bean-of-a-woman, with an exaggerated updo that was resembling the Leaning Tower of Pisa at the moment.

"Hello, Ruby," Abby said. "What can I do for you?"

"I need help. My do doesn't anymore. And I have a date tonight," she said, flopping into the chair by the window.

"If you don't mind waiting, I can work you in," Abby said.

"That will be fine. I'll just read some magazines, dear." Ruby reached toward the circular table for one and settled in for a spell.

A half hour later, Abby called Ruby over to her chair. "Let me disassemble the coif," she said, removing hairpins from the mass of red strands. "Then I'll shampoo you."

The mass soon collapsed past Ruby's shoulders, creating the illusion of a witch from a fairy tale who had been caught in a tornado while riding her broom.

"Time for the shampoo."

Ruby walked stiffly to the shampoo bowls, lowering herself

into the chair. "I need to bring my friend Penelope in here. She badly needs an update."

"Okay, Ruby. I'd be happy to help your friend."

Once Ruby was back in Abby's station, Abby asked what the occasion was.

"It's our wedding anniversary."

"How many years?"

"One big one. You don't know how many more there'll be at our age," Ruby said with a smirk. "He's a bit younger, but we are of that age where anything can happen."

"God didn't promise us another day, Ruby. Something can happen to any one of us, no matter our age." Abby dried the old woman's hair to damp, then brushed the curly hairs away from Ruby's face, toward the back of her head. She secured the mass of curls and, with hairpins, began anchoring her locks into an arrangement.

"That's true. Now, that one worries me," Ruby said, pointing toward Ivy, standing at the shampoo bowls washing someone's hair. "She's a pretty thing, especially since you jazzed her up. She could get into trouble."

"How so?"

"Too innocent. Not prepared for what life will bring her. And now she's lost weight. She's ripe for picking." Ruby spoke with authority and from experience, Abby guessed. But there was truth buried among her opinions.

Worry visited Abby regularly regarding Ivy. *At least, she's safe from her abusive mother.*

Ivy brought the client she had been shampooing to her station next to Abby.

Ruby looked over at her. "Honey, you look quite pretty. Abby did a nice job."

"Thank you," Ivy said, blushing.

"Are you dating?" Ruby asked.

"Yes, I have a boyfriend," Ivy said, letting a towel drop to the floor.

"You be careful with that boy."

Ivy looked surprised at the comment, and a little embarrassed.

"I'm sure Ivy knows how to handle herself, Ruby," Abby said, trying to intervene. But the thought had occurred to her more than once, that perhaps she needed to talk to the young woman. The points Ruby made were valid. Abby didn't know how much instruction Ivy had received from her mother. Perhaps none. Abby realized she needed to find time to have a talk with Ivy. And soon.

"You do such nice work, dear," Ruby said, patting Abby's hand, which was resting on her shoulder. "I look like a new woman. You erased twenty years from my face."

That wasn't exactly true. No amount of adjustments to her hair could reduce the wrinkles that had gathered together on the old woman's face. Abby noticed Ivy turn her head to hide the grin that sprang to her lips.

"I'll put you down for one week," Abby said as she wrote in the scheduling book. "And here's a card to remind you." She passed it to Ruby.

"Thank you, dear. Put Penelope down, too. I'll drag her in," she said as she slid several bills across the desk. "Keep the change."

"Thank you, Ruby. Here's a card for her, too. See you next week." Abby watched as Ruby glided out the door, in true model style. Through the glass she also saw a man she suspected was homeless. He seemed to be looking in the direction of the salon. Without a second thought, she walked out the door and across the street, just making the stoplight.

"Sir," she called when he turned away from her approach. "Please, may I talk with you?"

The man turned around, revealing a scraggly beard that was

partially gray. His brown hair grew past his collar in the back, while the front was wrapped over his ears. He appeared reasonably clean in jeans and a tee.

"Hi, I'm Abby," she said with a smile, reaching out her hand to the man.

He looked at her hand, and shook his head.

She stepped closer to him, dropping her hand. "That's my salon over there," she said, motioning. "A woman named Rose Tumbler used to sleep in front of the store. I let her; it's okay. Do you know her?"

He looked very uncomfortable and started to walk away.

Abby touched his elbow, and he jerked his arm from her.

"Don't."

"Okay. I'm sorry. Really, I mean no harm to you," she said rapidly. "I care about Rose and wondered if you knew her? That's all."

The man's eyes looked her up and down suspiciously, but he stopped moving away.

"You do know her, don't you?"

He nodded once.

"Do you know where she is? There was blood found at the entrance to my salon, so I'm worried about her." It wasn't reasonable to think this man had assaulted Rose. He was fragile in appearance, weakened.

He hung his head and shook it, no. Then he looked into her face and Abby saw sadness in his tired eyes. She wondered if he was sad because of Rose or his own circumstances.

"If you hear anything, would you let me know?"

He gave her a quick nod.

"Thank you." She smiled at the man, then extended her hand. This time he clasped it briefly. Silently, he walked on.

EIGHTEEN

"IVY, would you like to come upstairs to my apartment after work?" Abby asked. "You can meet Seely."
"Sure, cool." Ivy was organizing rollers in a plastic container. "I'd love to meet Seely."
"Good." Abby walked to the supply room to unpack a box of hair color. This was the time, while meeting the kitten, that she would have a talk with Ivy. She said a silent prayer for the correct words to come.

When Abby left the supply room, she saw Sonia lifting items on her station, putting them down, and continuing this action. Under her breath, she was mumbling in Spanish.

"What are you doing, Sonia?"
"Earrings!" she practically shrieked. "I can't find my earrings!"
"What do they look like?"
"Gold, big hoops," she replied, making circles in the air with her two index fingers beside her ears. "Tiny diamonds around. I took off to wash hair. Now, I can't find."

Ivy and Abby started searching for the lost earrings.

"Nothing over here," Ivy said from the shampoo bowls. "Could a customer have taken them?"

"It's possible," Abby said, looking through receipts on the desk. "We don't like to think such."

"*Ay caramba*," Sonia wailed. "My best. And I have a date."

"He won't know the difference," Ivy said innocently.

Sonia glared at Ivy and muttered in Spanish.

"Did you look in the trash?" Abby asked.

"No!" Sonia, uncharacteristically, got on her hands and knees to paw through her trash can. After a minute, she gave up.

"We'll keep an eye open for them, Sonia. Don't worry, they'll turn up somewhere," Abby said.

Looking in the mirror, Sonia let out an "eh" with a double hand gesture in the air beside her head. "No earrings!" She gathered her belongings and stomped toward the front door, mumbling in Spanish all the way.

"Have a good time, Sonia," Ivy called behind.

Sonia turned her head briefly toward Ivy, looking grumpy, then she was out the door.

"Let's go upstairs," Abby said, moving toward the door with her purse.

"Right behind you." Ivy grabbed her backpack.

The two women climbed two flights of stairs, puffing by the time they reached the top.

"Yikes, it's a good thing you aren't sixty," Ivy said.

"I agree. But I figure I'm getting exercise," Abby said with a smile.

She unlocked the door, and they went inside. Seely was quick to give them a vocal greeting.

"Aw, she's so cute," Ivy said, reaching down to pet the kitten. "Can I pick her up?"

"Sure. She's friendly." Abby deposited her purse and keys on the kitchen counter.

"Ooh, you are a darling girl," Ivy cooed into Seely's face. She let her backpack slide to the floor as she walked toward the couch. "You are so lucky, Miss Abby. She's wonderful."

Abby smiled from behind the counter. "I think so. I have no regrets."

"Someday, I'm going to get a pet. When I have my own place, that is." Ivy sat on the couch, continuing to caress the kitten. "I can't do it now, living at Mrs. York's."

"Would you like a soda or something else?"

"Yes, a soda. Thank you."

Abby came into the living room carrying two cans. She placed one in front of Ivy on the coffee table, then she sat next to the young woman. "You've lost weight, Ivy. The baby fat has disappeared."

"Yes! I'm so happy about that."

"What does your boyfriend have to say? What did you say his name is?"

"Scott. He likes it. Says I look really good," she said, snapping open the can.

"Hmm, I bet he does. Ivy, did your mother ever talk to you about having a relationship with a man? Such as, your right to say no?"

Ivy looked at her with questions in her eyes. "No? I guess. I don't remember."

"You don't have to go along with something that makes you uncomfortable. If Scott gets inappropriate, you can say stop. I hope you know that," Abby said, snapping open her can.

Ivy didn't respond.

She kept looking at Abby, so she continued. "Ivy, sometimes men think we want to go farther than we really do, and that's by how we respond to their advances. If we say no, they stop, or they should if they had a proper upbringing. But if we don't say stop or no, they continue. Then we can get into a very uncomfortable situation. We can even be forced into something, and that's called rape."

"I know what that is."

"Good. You don't want to put yourself in that sort of a situation, where you are forced."

"No, I don't want that to happen." Ivy absentmindedly caressed the kitten as she looked intently at Abby. "Scott wouldn't do that."

"I hope not."

"He wouldn't. He really likes me. A lot." Her eyes were so innocent, it melted Abby's heart.

"Have you two been intimate?"

"We kiss. A lot," she said with a grin.

"You do know how babies come about, right?" Abby asked.

Ivy laughed loudly. "Miss Abby, of course I do!" The kitten jumped off the couch. "I'm not that naïve."

"Okay. I was just asking. But be careful, Ivy. I don't want you to get into trouble."

Abby didn't know if she felt better after the conversation or not. Was Ivy getting the message, or was it too late? Had she rationalized their relationship into believing whatever they were doing was all right? Or was she being careful? Maybe she was worrying too much about this young woman she'd taken under her wing, professionally and personally. And maybe she was putting her nose into a situation that didn't need her attention. Abby also had to consider that what Ivy did was really none of her business.

"Have you seen your mother since the last incident?" Abby asked.

"No. I can't go around her. She'll beat on me again," Ivy said, shaking her head. "Maybe someday I can, but not soon."

"That's probably wise."

"Anyway, thank you for the soda and letting me meet Seely. She's a doll," Ivy said, standing. "I have a date with Scott, so I need to go."

"I'm glad you came in, Ivy. Have a nice evening," Abby said with a smile and a hug.

Ivy picked up her backpack from the floor as she walked out.

"Bye, Ivy," Abby said as the young woman walked down the stairs.

NINETEEN

MRS. YORK WALKED into the salon, looking like the epitome of a grandmother. With her white hair twisted back from her face and pink cheeks, she could have auditioned for a part in a play as Mrs. Claus.

"Hello, Mrs. York," Abby greeted.

Ivy waved at her from the shampoo bowls, sending a big smile as she cleaned the sinks.

"Good morning, dear," she said as she sat in Abby's chair. She smiled, her blue eyes crinkling.

"You look lovely today, Mrs. York. Blue really becomes you," Abby said.

"Thank you. I have a fondness for this blouse. It's comfortable, but not too warm for the summer heat."

Ivy walked toward the front door after she finished with the sinks. "I'm getting coffee. Anybody want some?"

A round of "no" was heard, so Ivy left.

Mrs. York and Abby walked to the shampoo bowls.

As soon as she was seated, Mrs. York spoke. "I'm concerned about Ivy."

"Oh? Why? Isn't she working out at your place?"

"She's a lovely renter, no problem there. I am quite fond of her. That's why I'm concerned."

"What's the problem?"

"A couple of nights, she didn't stay in her room." Mrs. York closed her eyes from the water spray. "I know she wasn't with her mother, so I presume she spent the night with her boyfriend."

"Oh, no."

"Yes, oh no. She's far too innocent, inexperienced to be behaving in that manner. So, I am telling you this in hopes you can talk to her."

"I already have. Recently."

"Hmm. Then she's in too deep already. You may not be able to get through to her," Mrs. York stated.

This was exactly what Abby was dreading. It wasn't that she was psychic, but this circumstance was predictable. As Ruby had wisely observed, Ivy was ripe for picking.

"I appreciate you talking with me about Ivy. I will see what I can do, if anything. If she's enamored with this guy, she's not going to listen," Abby said.

"I am afraid not."

Abby and Mrs. York returned to the chair as Ivy entered the door with her coffee.

Boisterous voices sounded as the officers congregated around the bar. It was Friday evening, and the sergeants, detectives, and other brass were gathered to celebrate a weekend off. Some had female companions, and others entered sporadically with women on their arms. Abby and Jack were at a side table, trying to carry on a conversation.

"This is a lively bunch tonight," Abby commented.

"Yeah, the weekends, or beginning of one, usually are loud,"

HAIRCUT AND HIGHLIGHTS

Jack said, taking a sip of his beer. "It's all good fun. The guys are just letting off steam."

"I can see that," she said with a smile.

"Jack!" a voice called out.

The couple looked up to see a man in a Hawaiian shirt and shorts, holding a mug of beer.

"Who's the lady friend?" he asked.

"This is Abby. Abby, Judge," Jack said, making introductions. "He's one of my detectives."

"Hi, Judge," Abby said to the man hovering a little too close.

"Abby, hey?" He looked at Jack and winked. "Nice to meet you, *Abby*."

She didn't understand the significance of the emphasis on her name. Maybe it was code for his approval …?

"Talked to an informant yesterday about that homeless woman," Judge said, directing his conversation to Jack. "He hasn't seen her or the boyfriend. Didn't know what happened at the salon, either."

"No one has seen her?" Abby asked.

"She owns the salon and knew the woman," Jack told Judge in explanation.

"No one I've talked to," he said to Abby. "Was she a friend?"

"Yes and no. I'm trying to help her get off the street."

"Good luck with that." Judge took a long drink from his mug.

"I'm getting lonely," said a female voice. A feminine hand slid into Judge's hand. All eyes turned on the woman standing tall in a green dress, exuding confidence.

"Oh, Sheila, this is Jack and Abby," Judge said. "My date, Sheila."

"Hi." Her voice was soft as rain, but her eyes were as mischievous as Abby's kitten. "I was getting lonesome over there all by myself." Sheila's eyes turned to Judge as she spoke.

Judge kissed her on the cheek. "I'm coming, honey." Turning

back to the seated couple, he said, "Gotta keep the lady happy. Nice meeting you, Abby. Jack, see ya around."

"They seemed nice," Abby said.

"Uh, yeah, I guess." Jack shrugged. "I don't really know her." Abby didn't think Judge had a steady relationship with Sheila. Not like Jack and her.

"Do you know any more about the blood or Rose?" she asked.

"A little. We haven't located her, but she's not in the morgue, hospital, or jail. No one fitting her description has shown up anywhere. Which is good news, don't you think?" he asked.

"How is that good news?"

"Well, she's not dead. We don't have a body, so she's likely alive," he said matter-of-factly.

"Not necessarily. Someone could have killed her *after* they murdered whomever on my doorstep. Maybe she saw something, so they killed her and hauled her body away, buried it in some woods or a backyard." Abby didn't look happily at Jack. "Someone could have stuffed her body in a burn barrel and set her on fire."

"My, you do have a vivid imagination," he remarked with a smirk.

"But it's true, isn't it?"

"I guess." He looked across the table at her. "Abby, you have to recognize that finding a homeless woman who doesn't want to be found is practically impossible. If she were a rotting corpse, it would be easier."

"So, you're saying you think she's alive?"

"It's likely."

"Then you have to find her." Abby gave him an insistent look.

"You don't understand," he said, scratching the side of his face. "She's homeless. Rose could have moved on, gone to Orlando, DeLand. Even out of state. Here's a hypothesis:

suppose she saw the murder go down. Whoever did it saw her looking. Bingo, she knows she's in trouble. Now Rose is scared, traumatized, and she leaves the area, afraid for her life. Isn't that reasonable?"

"Yes."

"We have no information to go on. The investigation is going to eventually die out in that case," Jack explained.

"Because she's homeless." It was a statement rather than a question.

"Partially."

"That's not fair."

"Yes, it is, Abby," he said, looking exasperated. "We have robberies of little old ladies to investigate. They want their belongings returned. We have assaults to investigate so the bad guys go to jail. Is it fair to leave them on the backburner so we can find Rose? A woman who doesn't want to be found?"

"You don't know that."

"Yes, I do. That comes from experience with the homeless."

"What if she's hurt? You saw the blood. It was everywhere."

"It wasn't her blood. And if she's hurt, she can go to the emergency room. Then we'd have a record of her," Jack said.

"What if she doesn't go?"

"Well, Abby, if she doesn't go, she could die. And then we'd find the body."

Abby twisted her mouth in frustration. She didn't like what she was hearing, so she looked away. Tears started to form in her eyes. Not really wanting to cry, she found she couldn't control the emotion.

"Abby, you are such a softy," Jack said, reaching a hand to touch her arm. "Please don't cry. I will keep a lookout for Rose. I'll keep asking homeless if they know where she is, even if the case is at a dead end. But you have to be reasonable about our resources."

"I understand," she said, wiping her cheeks with her hand. "I just had such hope for Rose."

"I know. You're a good person. Maybe too good."

She looked him in the face and gave a half smile. "It's okay."

"No more tears?"

"None."

"Okay then. Let's order dinner." Jack hailed the server.

TWENTY

AFTER ABBY RETURNED HOME, she had a thought about Rose. What if she was mad and avoiding her? Although, she couldn't imagine why she would be mad. All she had ever done is help her. Maybe she was still sleeping in front of her salon, but Abby hadn't caught her yet. After all, she'd only gone outside looking once. Abby set the alarm for four o'clock before going to sleep. Surely, if she was sleeping there, Rose would be in place by four.

When the alarm went off, Abby couldn't remember why she had set the alarm. When it finally dawned on her, she jumped out of bed, slipped her feet into shoes, and left her apartment wearing sweats. She glanced next door and didn't hear any sounds coming from the apartment, so she crept down the stairs as quiet as a burglar. Once at the door, she looked both ways to be sure no one was nearby. Seeing no one, she stepped out.

Abby walked around to the front of the salon. Rose was not there. Disappointed, she started to turn away and heard her name called. "Abby, what are you doing out here?"

Startled, she turned around to see Mark at the corner. He

was in full uniform, a handsome specimen to be sure. "Oh, you scared me!"

"I hope so. What are you doing out here at this time of night?"

"I-I, well, this will sound weird."

"Tell me anyway."

"There's a homeless woman who sleeps here. I let her. But one morning recently she wasn't there, and I found blood all over, so I called 911. I haven't seen her since and I'm worried about her," Abby explained, looking at him with concern.

"I heard about that from Sgt. Pardon. He knows I live here," Mark said.

It didn't surprise her that Jack and Mark knew each other. Cases had to overlap when there were injuries involved and other dangerous situations.

"Are you friends with this homeless woman?"

"Not exactly, but I was trying to help her. And now I don't know where she is."

Mark rubbed the back of his neck as if in thought. "I remember seeing her sleeping here a couple times. I didn't say anything to her."

"Her name is Rose. Rose Tumbler. She could be hurt."

"I'll remember, but I wouldn't count on finding her, Abby. The homeless move around. She could be anywhere," he said in a tender voice.

"So I've been told," she said with a sigh. "I'm trying to find her. I plan to ask at the churches downtown. Maybe someone knows where she is."

"It could be fruitless. Don't get your hopes up," he advised. "But you need to get back inside."

"Yes, I do." She was glad that homeless man she had seen outside her business didn't happen by. Abby turned toward the door and walked inside and up the stairs with Mark, until they reached their floor. Once there, she turned to him. "Thanks."

"What for? Telling you to go inside?" he smiled.

"No. For listening. Everyone thinks I'm being silly over some homeless woman. They don't understand that I care about her."

Mark regarded her for several seconds, then spoke. "You aren't being silly. You just have a big heart."

She dropped her head and thanked him again.

"Goodnight. What's left of it," he said, turning toward his apartment.

"Goodnight. Sleep well."

The next morning Sheila from the night before walked into the salon. Abby was surprised to see her. "Sheila! Fancy seeing you here!"

"Hello, Abby. I didn't know you worked here," she remarked, obviously equally surprised to see her.

"Actually, it's my shop. I own it."

"I wondered who had taken over after it closed," she said. "I used to come here, so I thought I'd stop in and see what's going on."

"Small world."

"Yes. Do you have any time? I need a trim."

"Yes, I have enough time until my next appointment. Follow me to the shampoo bowls."

Abby shampooed Sheila's long brunette locks, then wrapped a towel around her head before they returned to the chair. "Just a trim? Nothing more radical?"

"Nothing radical. My hair's gotten to a length where it wants to do funny things, so it's time for a trim. Maybe an inch?" she asked.

"Or two?"

"Whatever you think it needs."

Abby began sectioning off the woman's full head of hair.

After a while, Sheila began to talk. "So, you were with Jack last night. Nice fella."

"Yes, he is."

"Have you been seeing him long?" she asked.

"A few weeks. Do you know him? You didn't act like you did last night when we were introduced." Abby reached for the thinning scissors.

"I know him. I didn't want Judge to know how well," Sheila said, looking into the mirror at Abby's reflection. "You know what I mean?"

Abby's radar went up. Why didn't she want Judge to know she knew Jack?

"No, not really."

"You know he's a player, right?" Sheila asked.

"Who?"

"Jack."

"A player?"

"Yes, Jack is a player. You seem like a nice person, Abby," Sheila said. "You need to know who you're dealing with."

"Well, then, please tell me." She couldn't wait to hear the details.

"Jack loves the women. With his good looks, he has no trouble getting any woman he wants." She was having no difficulty sharing what she knew.

"So, I'm guessing you've been out with him?" Abby asked.

"Yes. Here and there, nothing steady."

"I see."

"Same as with Judge. Nothing serious, just go out for fun. But Judge doesn't need to know my business when I'm with someone else. I'm sure you understand," she said.

Sheila was painting a completely different picture of Jack than Abby had ever imagined. Which meant he was no boy scout, and not likely a faithful boyfriend.

Abby sliced her finger. "Ouch!"

"Cut yourself?"

"Hazzard of the job," she replied. "Excuse me while I get a BAND-AID."

Once in the backroom, Abby found the BAND-AIDs. And her self-control. As she ran her finger under cold water, she took a deep breath. So, was Sheila exaggerating? Could she be lying? Of course. However, to Abby she appeared simply to be chatting, not deliberately attempting a malicious attack. Abby wrapped a BAND-AID around her finger and returned to her chair.

"Are you okay?"

"Oh, sure. It's nothing. All of us cut our fingers. No big deal," Abby replied. "Where were we?"

"I was saying Jack is a player. I think he has commitment issues. Not unusual," she said with a knowing half smile.

"No, it's not. Men don't like to commit; women do."

"Some women, not me. That's why I like men such as Jack and Judge. I'm free to do as I please."

Abby had never held that mindset. She preferred steady relationships where she could trust the other person. Flitting around between several men was definitely not her style.

"I'm almost done. Do you want me to go any shorter?" Abby asked as she looked at Sheila's face in the mirror.

"It looks wonderful! You are *good!*" Sheila was all smiles as she looked in the mirror at her reflection. "Put me down for eight weeks. You're the only one who's going to touch my hair from now on."

Abby smiled too. "Okay. Let's get your cape off."

They walked to the desk where Abby accepted Sheila's money. "Do you prefer mornings or afternoons?" she asked, looking at the appointment book.

"Either."

"Here, let's go for one." She tapped her pencil by that time slot.

"Perfect. Thank you, Abby." Sheila flashed her a bright smile as she turned toward the door.

Another regular!

TWENTY-ONE

WHEN ABBY LEFT WORK, she walked to the Baptist Church nearby. As she approached, she saw numerous homeless people standing in line for dinner. So many, they were leaking out from the cafeteria. She noticed a woman who seemed to be organizing the people, so she approached her.

"Hi, I'm Abby Bugsly. I have a salon on Beach, where I allow one of the homeless women to sleep."

The woman graciously nodded her head, even though she seemed busy. "That's nice."

"She's been missing for a while, and I'm concerned. I thought maybe you would know her and may have seen her?"

"What does she look like?"

"About this tall," she said, holding her hand flat at the correct height. "Brown hair falling straight to her chin. She usually wears jeans or shorts with a tee. Of course, they all do that. She seems to be competent, not in a mental state. And her name is Rose Tumbler."

"That sounds like someone I may know," the woman said, waving her hand at the line of people to continue walking forward. "But I can't say if she attends these dinners or not."

"Why is that?"

"It's a matter of privacy."

"Oh. I was hoping …" Abby hung her head. "So, you can't tell me if you have seen her?"

"No, I'm not allowed. I'm sorry." The lines in her face drew close in concern.

"Okay. I guess all I can do is ask. Thank you for your time."

So much for the Baptist Church. On to the Methodist.

The two churches were close to each other, so she arrived in five minutes. There wasn't a line to eat, so she figured the Baptist had the duty that evening. She walked on the campus until she saw a man who looked like he belonged there. "Sir?"

"Hello, yes, can I help you?" he answered with a beautiful smile. He was bald, dressed in a suit, which was unusual for Florida during the summer months, and wore glasses. He looked like a pastor.

"Yes, I'm looking for a homeless woman named Rose Tumbler. She's about yay tall, brown hair to her chin. Dresses in jeans and tee-shirts. She's been missing for weeks."

"I know a Rose, but I'm not allowed to say anything," he said. "I'm sorry, but I don't have any information about her. Are you a relative?"

"No, I own the salon on Beach, and she sleeps there. I'm trying to help her get straightened out, but now she's been missing since I discovered the blood."

"Blood? What blood?"

Abby explained about the bloody mess she found at her doorstep.

"I see why you're concerned. That concerns me as well. I've had some talks with Rose myself, so I agree she has potential to straighten out her life. If she's alive."

"That's my biggest concern: *is* she alive?"

"I'll keep an eye out for her, try to guide her if possible."

"Would you let me know if you see her?"

"I can't do that. I'm only allowed to contact the police."

"Okay. Let me give you the name of the sergeant on the case. You can contact him if she shows up." Abby pulled out a business card, writing Jack's information on it. "I really appreciate this. Are you the pastor here?"

"Yes, I am. I'm Reverend Arnold," he said, extending his hand.

"So nice to meet you, Reverend. I'm Abby Bugsly."

"She's in God's hands, Abby."

"Yes, I know. I'm praying for her. Thank you, Reverend Arnold," she said in parting.

Abby walked home, feeling disappointed. The only other place to ask about Rose was the shelter on International Speedway. She would do that during the day when the administration was likely to receive people asking questions. Although, the police should have contacted them already, but she had to try. She had to satisfy herself that she had done all she could to locate Rose.

———

Around noon the next day, Abby parked her car in the lot outside the shelter. She walked past homeless people camping outside the gate, looking carefully at every face to see if one belonged to Rose. She walked to a woman standing behind a desk, introducing herself.

"I'm very concerned about a homeless woman who may be staying here," she said.

"Are you a relative?"

"No. I allow her to sleep at my place of business, and I've been trying to help her. But she disappeared after an incident where a lot of blood was found." Abby looked pleadingly at the stout woman in uniform. "I'm concerned if she's alive, all right, or whatever. I haven't seen her for weeks, which isn't like her."

The woman nodded like she understood. "A lot of people come here to see if their relatives are staying here. But due to privacy issues, we aren't allowed to say one way or the other."

"Even when a relative is asking?"

"Oh, yes. We don't know if the person asking wants to help or harm. Sometimes, it's a matter of abuse, so we are protecting the man or woman. We have no obligation to the person asking, only the one we shelter."

"That's very interesting, and I can see the wisdom there. I just want to help, but I see that I'm not going to be able to do that. Unless she contacts me." Abby pulled a business card from her purse. "I know you can't tell me if she's here, but if she is, or if she comes in, please give my card to Rose Tumbler."

"All I can say is maybe." But the woman tucked the card into a pocket, which gave Abby some hope.

"Thank you."

Abby passed by the gathering of campers, thinking she could ask them if they'd seen Rose. She asked the first three people standing near the gate. All of them turned their backs and walked away. It was obvious this was a tightknit group that protected each other. She wasn't going to get any information out of them. Jack had been right about that.

Abby drove back to her salon, feeling totally defeated.

"You did *what?*" Jack asked, visibly surprised.

"You heard me." Abby looked sternly across the table at him.

"I told you to let the professionals handle the investigation," he said, frowning at her.

"You aren't my father; you can't tell me what to do," she said, feeling the growing anger crawling up the back of her neck.

"I can tell you to mind your business when it comes to investigating a case," he stated, taking his mug into his hand. "You could have been hurt talking to those homeless people."

"I only talked to three outside the shelter. They weren't going to attack me there," she said, leaning forward a little.

"You went to the churches, too."

"So? I have a right to inquire about Rose. You aren't doing anything to locate her." She straightened up taller.

Jack's eyes grew dark. "We've talked to homeless people, or tried, been to the jail and shelter, churches, all of it. We already did it!" He took a swallow of his beer.

"And I checked also. Big deal," she said, slapping her napkin on her lap.

"It is a big deal. We investigated. We found nothing. End of story. You shouldn't have put yourself in harm's way for that woman," he said, softening his tone.

"Well, excuse me for caring." Her eyes flashed.

"I know you care, but you don't understand the homeless population. They think differently. They're always in survival mode, looking for opportunities. That's dangerous." He took another swallow.

"I wasn't wandering a homeless camp near the river. It wasn't dangerous where I was. Do I look like I got hurt? No, I don't," she said firmly. "I did nothing wrong."

"We're going to have to agree to disagree."

"Where Rose is concerned, we disagree."

"We sure do. I don't get why you care about her," he said, shaking his head.

"I don't get why you don't." She bored her blue eyes into him. "She's a human being."

"Well, that human being is on my list of worthless people." He placed his mug on the table with a clunk.

Abby sat back in her chair, staring at him in disbelief. She slapped her napkin on the table and pushed back her chair, standing. "I think we've said enough." She grabbed her purse from the floor and marched out of the restaurant.

"Wait!" he called out, but she kept going.

Flinging open the door, she stepped onto the sidewalk. She was only a few blocks from home, and with daylight savings time, it was still light outside. Abby felt perfectly safe walking home. However, she walked quickly on the chance Jack would follow. Considering he had to pay the bill, she felt she could get home before he caught up to her.

With every step she took, her anger grew. Every footfall added fuel to her flaming temper. *The idea, Jack telling me what to do!* After living with her husband, Abby wasn't about to allow another man to boss her around. And his attitude about Rose. *How insensitive, unfeeling!*

She turned the corner and saw a couple homeless women sitting on a doorstep. Abby nodded at them, smiled, and waved. They waved back. Pretty soon she rounded another corner, seeing her building at the opposite end of the block. She glanced back but didn't see Jack. Even so, she didn't slow her steps. Once at the building, Abby unlocked the door, and ran up the stairs as best she could. By the time she reached the third floor, she was puffing audibly. Once inside her apartment, she felt safe from any encounter.

TWENTY-TWO

ABBY WAS STILL REELING from the previous night's argument as she sat at her station, drinking coffee. Sonia was singing a Spanish song from her station as she arranged the items on top. She untangled the cord on the flatiron and then did the same with the curling iron. All the while Abby sat silently, thinking about Rose: where she was, how she was, would she ever come back?

Ivy jangled through the door, the bell swinging more than usual. Her expression was clearly upset.

Abby looked at her with curiosity. "You okay?"

Her eyes looked at Abby, then flooded with tears.

"Oh, honey, what's wrong?" Abby asked, rushing over.

Sonia stopped singing and cocked her head.

With her arms wrapped around Ivy, Abby guided her toward the backroom.

"Sit down in the chair. Do you want coffee? I can get you some."

"No. It makes me sick."

"Since when? You always drink coffee," Abby said.

"Since I'm pregnant," Ivy said flatly.

Abby was speechless. *Pregnant?*

Ivy looked up at Abby with big eyes. "Yes, I'm pregnant. You told me to be careful. I guess I wasn't careful enough." And again her eyes filled with tears and spilled over to run down her cheeks.

Abby sat heavily in the chair next to Ivy. "Wow," she said softly.

They were both sitting silently when Sonia walked in. She leaned against the doorjamb, looking at the two women. "What happen?"

Abby didn't know if she should answer or let Ivy, so she slid her eyes over to the girl.

The young woman looked over to Sonia and turned her lips down. "I'm pregnant."

"*Ay caramba!*" Sonia shrieked, grabbing both sides of her head, then spoke softly in Spanish, followed by a hearty foot stomp.

Abby sighed. She turned to Ivy. "You have support from me and Sonia. I hope you know that."

"Yes."

"*Si*, I support you," Sonia said, nodding her head.

"It's nice to know I have support. I sure don't have that from anyone else," she said, looking pitiful.

"What about your boyfriend?" Abby asked.

Ivy laughed dramatically. "He's gone. Soon as I told him, whoosh; he flew away like a heat-seeking missile."

Sonia and Abby linked gazes. They knew the big question hanging over their heads but were hesitant to ask.

"You have a lot to think about, decisions to make," Abby said. "If you need to come in late due to morning sickness or something, it's okay. We will cover."

"*Si*, cover," Sonia agreed.

"Thank you," Ivy said, shaking her head.

"You tell your mother?" Sonia asked.

"No! I'm not telling her."

"What about Mrs. York?" Abby asked.

"Not yet. But I will soon. I *have* to tell her," Ivy said. "She's been so nice to me. But I don't know how to tell her this news. A *baby!*" Ivy's eyes began to fill with sorrow again.

Abby and Sonia linked gazes again. They understood better than Ivy what the ramifications of a pregnancy could bring. Sonia had grown children, while Abby had none, but she knew the consequences facing Ivy. The poor girl had decisions to make, and none would be easy or without tears.

"Okay, ladies, we may have bad news to deal with, but we have a day ahead of us," Abby said. "Pull yourself together, Ivy, so you can meet the public. You can't solve anything today. Sonia and I will leave you alone now."

The two women walked out of the backroom, leaving Ivy to cry and compose herself. As they came through the pedi room to the front, Abby saw Jack sitting in the waiting area.

"Hey," he said.

"Hey."

"I have an appointment for a cut," he said with a slight smile.

"Really? I haven't checked the book yet." She felt awkward as she walked over to the book. "Yes, you sure do," she said after glancing at the book.

Jack stood and walked to her station. "You okay with this?"

"Sure, why wouldn't I be?" Abby would have to pretend everything was hunky dory.

As she washed his hair, she remembered the first time she had done this. She didn't have the same reaction as then. Once back in the chair, she drew out her shears and began snipping his locks. A fleeting thought ran through about shaving all his pretty curls away. *Serve him right.* But that wasn't professional behavior.

"I apologize for last night," he said, looking at her reflection in the mirror. "I was being insensitive."

"Yes, you were." She had no intention of letting him off easily.

"One thing you need to understand ... when you work in law enforcement, you tend to see people differently. We see the worst people, rarely the best, unless they're the victim. That colors our thinking and opinions." Jack paused. Abby didn't say anything, so he continued. "Frankly, I haven't met any decent homeless people. Maybe Rose is the exception, I don't know. I haven't interacted with her much. She might be very nice. You seem to think so."

"She *is* nice."

"Okay, then. She's nice. And you want to help her. I understand that you're that kind of person. That's great of you. But you have to understand that that is not my life experience." As he spoke, he looked steadily at her in the mirror.

"Don't you care about people?" she asked, gently trimming around his ear.

"Sure. Ones I associate with. Just not every person walking down the street."

"The guys you work with?"

"Definitely. And you."

Abby started feeling awkward again.

"I care what happens to you, so I don't want to see you used by Rose, or harmed by some homeless person," he said, staring at her in the mirror.

"I understand. I do," she nodded. "Our experiences are different. We see things based on experience, of course, from which we form our opinions."

"So, now that I've explained myself, will you forgive me?" he asked, giving her a boyish expression.

Abby couldn't help but grin. "Yes, I forgive you. Now, let me explain a few things."

"Shoot."

"I was raised in church. I was taught values and to love

people, so I do my best to live up to standards. Helping Rose comes naturally. But I'm not a fool, Jack," she said as she reached for the electric razor. "I have seen the dark side of a person, been the victim, and have the scars to prove it. That experience taught me a great deal about men."

"You don't trust men?"

"It depends on the man. I don't lump all men in one category; I'm discerning. I give everyone the benefit of the doubt at first. But harm me, hurt me, I'm not going to be a doormat. I don't tolerate bad behavior."

"Do you forgive?"

"In my heart, I forgive the person, but I'm done with them. Maya Angelou said, 'When people show you who they are, believe them the first time.'" Abby brushed the back of his neck free from hair.

"I see."

Abby looked at Jack through the mirror. "Your curls are all done."

"Looks great. Thanks, Abby." Jack stood, then smiled at her. "Are we okay?"

"We're okay."

"Are you free for a burger and a movie tomorrow?"

"That sounds nice."

"I'll come by around six."

"I'll be ready."

TWENTY-THREE

"I SHOULD HAVE STAYED FAT," Ivy said as she dug into her salad. "He never paid any attention to me until I lost weight."

"I don't know what to say to that," Abby said, moving the lettuce around in the bowl with her fork.

"I told Mrs. York."

"Oh, good. I was going to ask." It had been almost three weeks since Ivy announced the big news about the baby.

"She was really sweet about everything. She even said I could still live there with the baby if I keep it." Ivy looked off at nothing.

"That was very nice of her. I hate to ask this, but *have* you decided to keep it?" Abby waited to hear the answer, stopping her fork's travel to her mouth midway.

"I don't know. My first thought was to get rid of it, but that isn't something I can do."

"I'm glad to hear that."

"I can't do that. So, I have to decide if I want to give it away for adoption or raise a child," she said, then sighed deeply. "This is an awful decision to make. Either way, I could regret the choice."

"Ivy, have you thought that you don't have to make a decision right now? You have time to adjust to this new reality before making a choice that will affect you and another life," Abby said, resuming her eating.

"I suppose you're right. I hadn't thought about it that way. I don't have to make the biggest decision of my life immediately, do I?" Ivy's face perked up at that thought.

"No, honey, you don't." Abby smiled sweetly at the young woman across the table. "Take your time. Do you pray?"

"Pray? Uh, maybe sometimes." Her expression didn't indicate it was a familiar practice.

"I would suggest praying about the decision. As they say, take it to the Lord in prayer."

"I can do that." Ivy shoved a mouthful of lettuce into her mouth. After chewing, she asked, "What do you think I should do? Keep it or adopt it out?"

"Oh, Ivy, honey, I am not making that decision for you. I don't even want to make a suggestion what you should do because that would be my opinion. This is your decision to make because *you* have to live with that decision. Whichever way you choose, the baby will be brought into this world. That's a good thing. And I know you'll make the right choice." Abby cast her eyes into the salad to avoid looking at Ivy.

"You're right. *I* have to decide." Ivy gave Abby a bright smile. "Thanks for being there for me."

"No problem, honey."

Abby heard a firm knock on her door as she washed the dinner dishes. Jack was working, so maybe it was Mark next door? She eagerly walked to the door and flung it open.

"Hello, Abby."

It wasn't Jack or Mark who stood in the hallway. It was Eric Straus, her ex-husband.

"What are you doing here?" she asked, her throat beginning to tighten. First, a homeless man is hanging around her business, now a visit from her ex. What was happening?

"That's not a friendly greeting for your husband," Eric said, giving her a slow smile.

"Ex. *Ex*-husband. We're divorced."

"Just a piece of paper. Aren't you going to invite me in?" he asked, his seductive smile growing.

"You don't need to come in. What do you want?"

"Now, sugar, how am I going to tell you that, standing in the hall? Do you want your neighbors to hear our business?" he said as he pushed past her into the apartment. "Hey, not bad," Eric's eyes scanned the place.

Abby kept the door open as a precaution. She turned around and looked at her ex-husband through glaring eyes. *"What do you want?"*

"Wow, such an attitude, sugar." Eric laughed, then moved toward the couch. "I'm going to get comfortable right here," he said, sitting his lean body on the furniture.

Abby decided to remain standing. Most people thought she was a nice person and caring, no doubt forgiving. But she hadn't forgotten Eric's abusive ways. How he belittled her, even in front of their friends. How he could turn on a dime and scream hurtful words. Then there were the times he was physical. She shook her head to free those memories. Eric did not deserve a friendly welcome. She was better off standing than sitting, just in case.

"So? You're here because …"

"What's your hurry? Got a hot date or something? Am I messing up your love life?" he asked with a smirk.

"None of your business. Why are you here?" she asked again.

"I was in town. You do remember my parents live in

Daytona Beach? While I was visiting them, I thought I'd drop by and say hi to my ex." He couldn't have smiled wider if he tried. Still the same charmer; no doubt the same jerk, too.

"Hi. Now, you can leave." She crossed her arms across her chest.

"Whoa, slow down a minute. I just got here. Come sit by me," he said, patting the couch. "I promise I won't bite. I just want to see how you're doing."

"I'm doing great. No doubt you saw I opened a salon downstairs, so I am gainfully employed. Life is good," she said, raising her eyebrows up and down. "And you?"

"The same. Still employed by the same people, steady income as before. Living in the same house you and I shared. Nothing much has changed, except you're not there."

Eric ran his fingers though his curly brown hair. Clean shaven, he had been considered dreamy in high school. But that was decades ago. Overindulgence in alcohol showed around his eyes, and his face was flushed. He may not have had a drink yet but he wasn't off the hooch, judging by his appearance.

"I'm making friends again, getting to know the stores and restaurants. Life is good here. I'm very glad I moved back. I even have a kitten," she said as she spied Seely coming out to the living room.

"A cat. Uh. Don't come this way, cat. I'm allergic." Eric waved his hand at the kitten to suggest it not venture forth. But it did anyway.

"Seely, come here," Abby said. The kitten listened for a change and walked to her rather than to Eric. She picked up her cat and held it so it didn't bother him.

"Thanks." He watched her as she cooed to the feline in her arms. "So, no boyfriend?"

"I told you that isn't any of your business."

"I was just thinking, you know, we could, umm, for old time's sake ..."

"No way." Abby put down the kitten, then placed both hands on her hips. "Isn't it time you left? You weren't invited. I think it's time you leave. Like, *now*."

"Okay, okay," he said as he got up from the couch. "You didn't even offer me something to drink. Bad hostess."

"Leave!"

"Yeah, yeah." Eric walked to the door. "You haven't changed at all."

"And neither have you. Get out!"

"I'm going, see?" He stood in the doorway. "I'm gone. See ya again, sometime." With those parting words, he walked out and shut the door behind.

Abby was shaking; she wasn't sure whether from rage or fear. The audacity of Eric, thinking he could just drop in at will! But what *really* disturbed her was the possibility he could return.

TWENTY-FOUR

FUMING, Abby looked for a way to calm herself. The tea she'd fixed hadn't done the trick. She decided enough time had passed since Eric left that she could safely walk around the block, pound her anger into the cement. She bounced down the stairs to the outside, full of adrenalin.

"Yes, this is good," Abby thought as she swiftly stomped along the sidewalk. *One foot in front of the other, leave the negative behind.* She walked several blocks away, somewhat near the Cuban restaurant where she and Jack had dined. As she swung her arms in time with her pace, she noticed a couple ahead, holding hands. From the back, she did not recognize the woman. However, from the back she most definitely recognized Jack. Stopping abruptly, she stared at the couple walking. *What?*

They stopped at the next alley, turned toward each other, and kissed. And it was a long, sloppy kiss. Abby felt her stomach clench. She quickly turned left at the corner to avoid being seen. Sheila had been right. Jack was a womanizer. How long had that display been going on? And did it matter, the amount of time? Not really. He was a cheat.

Abby's feet were on fire now, fueled by what she had seen.

HAIRCUT AND HIGHLIGHTS

Men! Gritting her teeth, she charged ahead, pounding the surface under her feet. *Do I have stupid written across my forehead? First Eric, now Jack.*

She came to her building and took a peek at the doorway to see if anyone was there. It was vacant, so she went upstairs to her apartment. *What a miserable night!*

Abby was taking a break at her station. As she lounged in the chair, she glanced over at Ivy. She looked pregnant, with a baby bump poking out under her clothes. Just a month ago she had shown no outward signs. She remembered plenty of incidents where Ivy had run to the restroom and looked green when she returned. Abby wondered if Ivy was farther along than originally thought.

Suddenly, Sonia shouted out in Spanish, causing everyone to look at her. She jumped up and down with excitement, still squealing her joy.

"What happened, Sonia?" Abby asked.

"Earrings! I found earrings!" In her hand, she clutched a large pair of hoops with diamonds sparkling.

"Where were they?" Ivy asked.

"I find stuck to bottom of roly-poly." What she meant was the roll-around black utility carrier they all used to store their curlers, hairpins, and such.

"Stuck? When did you clean it last?" Abby asked, wondering what gummy substances might be there.

Sonia rolled both hands in the air. "No know."

"You might want to clean that, Sonia," Abby suggested, pointing at the carrier.

"*Si.* I clean. But happy, happy, I find earrings!" Sonia smiled so brightly.

Abby rolled her eyes as she waited for Ruby to arrive. When

she entered, Ruby had her friend Penelope beside her. Penelope Hardwood was an original. Up in years, she dressed as if she lived in Alaska, wearing a heavy sweater during the days of highest heat. Compared to Ruby, she was a prudish, droopy daisy. The woman appeared dowdy in her loose-fitting, blue housedress, the epitome of frumpiness. Abby quickly understood why Ruby was bringing her in for an update. She really needed it. Her gray hair stood out from her face in a halo of frizz.

"Ah, this must be Penelope," Abby said with a warm smile.

"Yes, Penelope, this is Abby. She's amazing," Ruby stated.

Ruby was all smiles, decked out in an orange jumpsuit that clashed severely with her red hair. She walked like the model she used to be. Abby couldn't help but grin.

"Well, Miss Ruby," Abby said, "step over to my chair."

Ruby did as requested.

"You seem very sunny today." She started to disassemble the old woman's hair.

"Child, I feel like I'm newborn." Ruby crossed her long legs. "You know how it is: a little rumble under the sheets can put a smile on your face the next day. Every pore in my body is tingling, every nerve is relaxed. I am in bliss."

Abby glanced around to see who had heard Ruby's statement. Apparently, everyone, because they all had smirks or smiles on their faces. The woman was pushing ninety-five and here she was talking about sex! Abby found that amusing and remarkable. Apparently, her friend was embarrassed because Abby could see her sitting in the chair, her face bright red.

"Isn't life grand?" Ruby asked, receiving the cape Abby placed over her.

"Yes, Ruby, with you around life is certainly grand."

After finishing with Ruby, Abby escorted Penelope over to her chair. She fingered the old woman's frizz. "You can tame this by using product. I think a little cut would help, too. What do you think?"

"I guess so."

Penelope seemed hesitant, so Abby turned to Ruby who stood beside her. "Ruby, what do you think?"

"Definitely cut it. It's way too long for a woman her age," Ruby said, mincing no words. "And get rid of that frizzy head of hair."

Penelope looked across at her friend with wide eyes.

"That sound okay to you?" she asked Penelope.

"What Ruby said."

"Okay, then away we go." Abby shook the cape out to place around Penelope.

An hour later, Penelope was a new woman. Her hair curled softly around her face, bringing out her blue eyes. There was no frizz for a change.

"Didn't I tell you Abby is amazing?" Ruby asked.

Penelope nodded her head and smiled shyly. "Thank you."

The two old ladies left the salon with a spring in their steps.

The time rolled by slowly because Abby did not have a full book that day. But she still had one more client, and it was Jack. She was not done fuming from last evening's discovery. She didn't know how she was going to handle the situation.

"Hi, there!" Jack said as he walked in the door, jolly, and all smiles.

"My, you certainly are in a good mood," Abby remarked as Jack sat in her chair. Maybe he and Ruby had experienced the same thing last night?

"Yeah, life is good. You'll hear no complaints coming from me. Now I'm going to relax into this chair so my favorite hairdresser can trim my curls. Yeah, I feel great."

Abby felt like taking the cape and tightening it around his neck. *How dare he be so happy after making me so angry?* She washed his hair, refraining with difficulty from turning the spray nozzle into his face.

Once back at her station, Jack became chatty. "I love this time of year. It's getting cooler, the nights aren't humid, and it's just a great time to be outside. I love walking in the evening in downtown. So peaceful."

Yeah, like you were doing last night. "Um-hm." Abby kept cutting his curls, all the while thinking what a jerk he is. If he knew what she had seen last night, he wouldn't be so chatty about it.

"I just feel so peaceful and relaxed. A walk in the evening does that for me," he said, a small smile tugging at his lips as he appeared to reminisce.

"Um-hm." If he'd shut up for a moment, he'd have noticed that Abby's eyes were sparking with anger. She glanced at her reflection in the mirror. She was easy to read, but she couldn't help it. Her anger was bordering on rage as she listened to Jack prattle on.

"Oh, I have to tell you, we can't go out tonight as planned," he said as she picked up the electric razor. "Something has come up that I have to attend. Sorry, but we can go out another time"

Something has come up? Abby knew exactly what that "something" was. "Really? How interesting. I wonder if it has anything to do with that woman I saw you with last night?"

Jack's mouth dropped to his chest and his eyes widened.

"Yes, I saw you last night. I saw you kiss that woman at the alley," Abby told him so he knew for certain she had seen him. "You, Sergeant Jack Pardon, are a jerk and a cheat."

With the last word out of her mouth, she guided the razor up the back of his head and over the crown until she had created a ditch in the center of his head. Jack shrank in the chair as he looked in horror at a three-inch-wide center part carved from his neckline to his forehead. His hands flew to his head and touched what looked like a reverse mohawk.

"My *hair*! My *curls*! What did you do?" he gasped.

"It's pretty obvious what I did, Jack." Abby looked at him with no sign of regret. "Now, take your butt out of my salon and don't ever come back."

Jack looked over his shoulder in astonishment at Abby. "You're a flaming psycho!"

"And proud to be so."

Hearing applause from the women in the salon, he quickly stood, ripped the cape from his neck, and flung it behind as he stumbled his way out the door, eager to get away from her. A few bravos were shouted, while some of the women laughed at the site of Jack's hair.

"Abby?" Sonia asked, looking at her boss, horrified.

"It's okay. He had it coming," she stated, wiping her hands together to indicate her satisfaction. "Job well done, if I do say so myself." Abby smiled.

TWENTY-FIVE

ROSE TUMBLER WALKED past the campers outside the gate, then entered the building. When she approached the desk, she was a willing candidate—this time.

"Hi," she said to the woman behind the desk.

"You look familiar. Have you been here before?" she asked.

"Yes, but just overnight."

"I seem to remember you disappeared before your appointment for evaluation," the woman said, adjusting her glasses.

"Yes, I did that."

"What brings you here today?"

"I want to get in your program."

"You do? Why? What changed from last time?" she asked, reaching for a clipboard.

"Uh, I'm afraid. And it's time."

The woman looked at her with more seriousness. "Afraid of what? Or is it whom?"

"No one in particular. I'm just scared being on the street," Rose lied, feeling ill at ease. She was afraid for her life, not that she could give the real reason for her fear. No one snitched, ever. "I lost my boyfriend, so I need to get off the street. He was my protection. I don't want to do this anymore."

"What is your name?"

"Rose Tumbler," she said. "Please help me."

The woman looked kindly at her. "Rose, we will help you. I just need information from you."

"I know. Identification. I have that," Rose said, reaching in her back pocket for her driver's license. She slid the license across the desk to the woman, noticing the name on her badge said Nancy. "Nancy, please help me." Tears formed in her eyes as she looked at the woman.

"Oh, child, you are safe here," she assured her, reaching out a hand to touch Rose's arm. "No one will harm you here, and no one will even know you're here. You're safe now."

"Thank you," Rose said in a choked voice.

"Many homeless don't have any I.D.," she said, examining the license. "Let me ask you a few questions, and then we'll get you a cot, okay?"

"Sure."

After a few minutes, Rose was shown to her cot, which was down the opposite side from where she'd been the last time.

"Cot ten is yours," Nancy said. "I'm sure you remember where the dining area is located, and the bathrooms."

"Yes, I do."

"You can get cleaned up any time between now and dinner. Just shove your bag into one of the lockers in the hall, okay?"

Nancy was a nice lady, and Rose appreciated her kindness more than she could express.

"Thanks, Nancy."

"Chicken potpie is for dinner. You'll like it," she said. "Peach cobbler for dessert."

"Sounds good."

"I'm going back to the desk. If you need me, that's where I'll be." Nancy left Rose alone.

Sitting heavily on the cot, Rose breathed a sigh of relief. She was safe. While she hadn't felt unsafe living on the street, she had always been cautious, never taking unnecessary chances with people she didn't know. But then, she deliberately hadn't made many friends. She preferred to be alone. Except for Sam. She quickly recognized the necessity for having protection the first night on the street. Rose didn't sleep that night for fear someone would take her belongings, such as they were. Or do worse. She was a female, alone and unprotected. She wouldn't be capable of fighting off a man. Unless she had a man.

The next day she met Sam. He was close in age, not bad looking, with his mop of blonde dreadlocks. What was more important, he was large in stature. He took an immediate interest in her, and she did not thwart his attempt to be friendly. Sam was her protection from that day forward. It wasn't until recently that she found herself alone again after Sam was arrested for trespassing in a church parking lot. So, she found a safe haven at the storefront of Goldilocks until he returned.

Rose didn't do drugs and didn't appreciate being around people who did. Some of them got nasty, others just sat in a stupor. She didn't want to be hit up for money so someone could buy drugs, either. The farther away she was from that scene, the better. She had also managed to avoid being around violence all this time, thanks to Sam. Rose had experienced enough violence during her childhood. Anything that smelled like violence sent her reeling. And then Sam returned, bringing the worst violence she had ever experienced. That was the catalyst that brought her to the homeless center.

She couldn't deal with the homeless situation anymore. It was too risky with her being alone, not to mention, witnessing that murder. Yes, she'd witnessed a murder, right there at what she thought was her safe haven. She couldn't live needing to constantly look over her shoulder. It was time to get her act together; return to society, if it would have her. She knew Abby would help her. But first, she had to go through this program.

As promised, dinner consisted of chicken potpie. And it was yummy, by Rose's standards. The peach cobbler that followed was also very good. Everyone around the table seemed to appreciate what was served. There were not a great many staying, judging by the attendance at dinner. Probably because of the weather, which was cooling down. Much more comfortable to sleep outside now. During the winter months, Rose was sure the center would be jammed.

Rose retired early. She hoped her roommates on either side of her were more agreeable than the last time when they were feuding. She didn't want to wake to another surprise.

Settling into the cot, she felt the need to pray. No one was in the room to bother her, so she said silent prayers of gratitude. It had been a while since she had prayed. Heck, it had been a while since she had done a lot of things most people considered normal and took for granted. Living on the street wasn't conducive to prayer. And there wasn't much to be grateful for, except still being alive. Unlike her boyfriend being cut up that night.

Rose didn't see how Sam could have lived through that attack, judging by the amount of blood she saw. Yes, she was very grateful to be in this cot, in the center, with a full belly, and clean clothes on her body. However, she mourned the loss of Sam. Poor Sam. But if he hadn't come back, those two men might have killed her, thinking she was somehow involved in what Sam did, whatever *that* was. She never knew his business. So, instead, Sam paid the ultimate price. And she was alive. *Thank you, Lord.*

―――

The next morning, Rose enjoyed breakfast, especially the coffee. It wasn't too strong, nor was it weak. The scrambled eggs were moist, not overcooked, and the sausage patties were cooked through. Delicious! If she started all her days this way, she would consider herself blessed.

At eleven o'clock, Rose sat with a counselor in a small office. She was attractive, nicely coifed, manicured hands, and clothes that looked like they came from Macy's. The counselor was a shining example of what women like Rose should aspire to be. Was that possible after all Rose had been through?

"I am Lori Waxmeyer; you can call me Lori," she said with a smile.

"Okay, Lori." Rose felt reasonably comfortable with the counselor.

"Now, we need to ascertain where you are currently and where you need to go in the future so we can direct your course," she began, leafing through some papers. "Are you on drugs? It's all right to tell me. You won't be arrested."

"No drugs."

"What about alcohol?"

"I drink sometimes." Rose paused, then began again. "It's not that I have to, but lately I've been sad. I get a little buzz and I feel better."

"I see. Do you consider yourself an alcoholic?"

"No. Definitely not." She knew what the alcoholics looked like on the street. They were loud, walking around unbalanced, and most of them became mean when they'd had a snoot full.

Lori wrote everything on paper that Rose said, then asked, "Did you graduate high school or college?"

"High school."

"What skills do you have? For example: typing, computer knowledge, factory worker."

"I went to work immediately after high school in an office. Yes, I type. I can use a computer."

"Those are good skills. You should be employable, Rose," Lori said with an encouraging smile.

Rose nodded, not knowing how to respond. *Who hires a former homeless woman?*

"With those skills, you won't have to be trained for a job, unless you don't want to work in an office."

"An office is okay."

"Do you have any other aspirations? What did you want to be when you were a child?"

"A chef," she answered.

"We can look for a cooking job for you if you'd rather. You can take some courses to train."

"I'd like that. But let's go with the office job. I can go to school later to be a cook if I decide that's something I'd like to do."

"Okay, I'll look into that for you," she said with a smile.

"Yeah, about that. How does that happen? It's not that I don't want to improve myself, but I've been living a completely different life. How do I switch over?" Rose asked.

"I understand. The transition will take some time and effort on your part. It doesn't happen overnight. You're used to this," she said, using cupped hands to demonstrate, "and now you are asking to be over here." She moved her cupped hands a foot to the left. "You'll be in counseling, so you can adjust to the changes, and be taught some life skills also."

"Okay." *Counseling? Whatever it takes.*

"At some point, we'll get you an interview for a job."

"I don't have decent clothes."

"No one does, Rose. We'll provide clothes."

"Okay."

"Do you have any questions?"

"When do I have to leave and get my own place? When I have a job?" Rose asked.

"You live here until you graduate to transitional housing.

That's after you have a job. We save the money you earn once you are employed, until you can take care of yourself. We don't throw you out. We want you to be self-sufficient before you leave us." Lori gave her an encouraging smile.

"That sounds good." Rose couldn't believe what she was hearing. These people who she didn't know were going to take care of her, help her get on her feet. No one had ever helped her during her entire life, until Abby came along. Now, Rose had a group behind her, working to straighten out her life. Her prayers had been answered.

TWENTY-SIX

Three Months Later

IVY WADDLED INTO THE SALON, fatigue clearly showing in her face. Her tummy significantly pushed out the voluminous shirt she was wearing over her pregnancy jeans as she continued the trek to her station.

"Good morning, Ivy," Abby said.

Ivy rolled her eyes over to her boss. "What's good about it?"

"Oh, it's that kind of day, huh? What's wrong?"

"Name it, and you'll have your answer."

"How is your back? Still hurting?"

"Of course. It never stops."

"Poor baby," Abby said. "You can go to the pedi room and turn on the massager, if you like."

"Yeah, I'll do that." Ivy waddled toward the room.

"Poor mama," Sonia said as she backcombed her client's hair.

"She looks ready to pop," said the client.

"*Si*, I think."

"Me thinks, too. She's much farther along than we thought,"

Abby commented, then walked toward the pedi room. "Ivy, just how far along are you?" she asked as she stood in the doorway.

The young woman opened her closed eyes while she relaxed in the chair. "I'm not sure."

"I think you know and you're not telling me," Abby pressed. "Your doctor would know and certainly has told you."

Ivy sighed and threw up both hands in resignation. "Okay. He thinks I'm around eight months."

Abby stared at her briefly before speaking, doing calculations in her head. "Ivy, it hasn't been that long since you were with your boyfriend."

"Yeah, I know. I think it's the guy before him who got me pregnant," she said sheepishly.

"*Before* him? Ivy, I thought that guy, what's his name, was your first experience?"

"Yeah, I know what you thought. He wasn't. And his name is Scott. There was a guy before that. George," she said, releasing a groan. "He's the daddy."

"You lied to me."

"Not exactly. I just didn't tell you everything," Ivy said with a shrug.

"That's a lie by omission."

"Whatever."

"Whatever?" Abby pulled a pedicure stool closer to the machine and sat on it. Looking at Ivy, she said, "Now it makes sense why Scott bolted, although he might have done so anyway. He certainly wasn't interested in being responsible for another guy's baby. Ivy, you should have told me."

"I didn't want you to think I was a bad girl," Ivy said, her bottom lip beginning to quiver.

"I don't think you're a bad girl. I think you're naïve. Didn't you use protection? Or think to be on the pill?" she asked.

"It was only one time. *Once!* I didn't think anything would happen."

HAIRCUT AND HIGHLIGHTS

"As I said, naïve. Once is all it takes."

"Obviously. I know that now. At first, I thought the baby was Scott's because we did it more. Turns out it wasn't," she said, rolling her eyes.

Abby sighed and shook her head. "Nothing can be undone. Have you decided what you're going to do?"

"Yes. I'm keeping the baby," Ivy said firmly.

"Okay. You do realize your life is going to drastically change? No nights out partying. The baby comes first, always. And if you think you're tired now, just wait till you have sleepless nights due to the baby." Abby cocked her head to the side, looking for Ivy's response.

"Mrs. York has been filling me in on what to expect," Ivy said, rolling her bottom lip under her teeth. "She gave me some books to read. Said she'd help with the late-night feedings."

"That's very sweet of her. But you can't allow her to do everything. You, my dear, are the mother and the one who should be up at two a.m. feeding the baby, not Mrs. York."

"I know, I know. Don't pick on me," Ivy said, looking at her with emotion rolling across her face. "She said she'd help, not do everything. I'll get up. You're right, it's my baby. I will take care of it."

"I hope so. Otherwise, you need to give it up for adoption if you don't think you can handle the responsibility." Abby raised her eyebrows to emphasize the point.

"*No!*" Ivy declared firmly, looking like she was ready to cry. "I really want the baby. And she'll love me, like my mother didn't."

"I see." Abby paused, recognizing why Ivy wanted to keep the baby. "You said 'she'. Is it a girl?"

Ivy's face brightened. "Yes, I'm having a girl." Happiness exploded over her face. "A little girl; just what I've always wanted."

"That's wonderful, Ivy. I'm happy for you." Abby truly was

pleased for Ivy, but didn't think, regardless of the denials, that she was prepared to care for a baby. Ivy would have to discover that for herself. Or maybe surprise everyone.

Ivy settled back into the chair for more massage, but Abby had more questions.

"Have you told your mother she's going to be a grandmother?" she asked.

"Nope," she said, not opening her eyes. "I haven't seen her, talked to her, nothing."

"Don't you think she should at least know? She doesn't have to see the baby or be involved in any way."

"Nah-uh. Not happening." She still didn't open her eyes.

Abby didn't know how to pursue that and thought it best to let it drop. "Your choice," she said, turning to walk back to the customer area.

Since Abby didn't have a customer at the moment, she decided to sanitize her combs. As she gathered them into her hands, she heard the bell tinkle. When she looked over to see who it was, she was surprised. There stood her ex-husband. Again.

"What are you doing here?"

"I came to see you," he said, all smiles.

"Once was enough. Leave."

Instead of leaving, Eric walked further inside, acting like he held ownership to the business. He cast his eyes around, nodding, and smiling at some of the ladies staring at him.

"Eric, I asked you to leave."

"I'm not ready," he said, hands on his hips.

"Oh, maybe you want a haircut?" she asked, returning the combs on her station and picking up a pair of scissors. "That can be arranged." She wore a devilish smile on her face. "It would be my pleasure to cut your hair."

Eric turned to look at her directly. "Oh, no, I'm not letting you near my hair. You think I'm crazy?"

"Maybe." Abby advanced toward him, still wearing a devilish smile.

"Hey, what are you doing?" Eric moved to the side.

"You'll see."

Eric sprinted away from her, trying to put space between them. He ran around the display case with the products for sale. Abby kept coming. The women began to chuckle and some applauded.

"Get him, Abby!" one lady called out.

"Give him a buzz cut," said another.

"Shave him bald!" shouted still another lady.

Looking quite nervous, especially now that Abby was being encouraged, Eric made haste to the front door. On his way past Abby's station, he slipped on some loose hair she hadn't swept up. Down he went, on both knees. A burst of laugher rang out from all the women as he crawled to his feet. With several long strides, he was out the door. Hearty applause followed him.

Abby placed the scissors on her station and wiped her hands together. "Good riddance."

———

The Chat had been rolling along from talk of Hillary's boyfriend still being around to why Jack and Abby were no longer dating to the whereabouts of Rose.

"So, you never saw your homeless woman again?" Latisha asked. "It's been months since she disappeared, hasn't it?"

"Yes. About four. And no one sleeps in my doorway after that incident," Abby replied, stirring her coffee. "I think everyone's scared to sleep there."

"Makes sense," Latisha said.

"You never found out anything?" Bobbi asked.

"A little. Mark, the fireman, you know, my neighbor? He told me they had found a body a couple weeks ago. It was a man and he had been cut up badly. According to Mark and the police, he is the blood match to all that blood found on my doorstep." Abby looked from one face to the other as she spoke. "Now we at least know who the victim was, and for sure it wasn't Rose's blood."

"So, who was the man they found?" asked Bobbi.

"A homeless man known as Sam. His blonde dreadlocks helped to identify him. He was Rose's boyfriend."

"This means Rose is alive," Hillary stated.

"I would think so. Unless something else happened to her." Abby couldn't imagine why she hadn't been contacted if she were still alive.

"Very strange," Hillary said.

"She's a homeless person. Those types pick up and move on a whim, let alone with a murder happening right where she slept," Latisha said. "I'll bet she left town. Wouldn't blame her."

"That doesn't explain her not contacting me," Abby said.

"I think you put too much importance on your so-called friendship," Latisha continued. "Homeless don't think that way. It's all about survival. She's long gone, looking for another handout. Someone to use."

Bobbi looked at Latisha, then Abby, and back to Latisha. "Abby tried to help Rose. She's invested. I understand her concern. She'd like to at least know for sure she's alive."

"Humph. Whatever."

"And Jack has never called you since the haircut?" Hillary asked.

"No. And that's fine with me. He's a cheater."

"I kinda hinted he was. That was my suspicion, anyway," Hillary said. "He sure looked weird running around with a reverse mohawk. Can you imagine the ribbing he took from the guys?" she grinned.

Everyone laughed.

TWENTY-SEVEN

"TELL me why you're afraid. You mentioned that early on and haven't said much since. I think it's more than being on the street without your boyfriend," Lori said.

Rose looked down at her clean hands and nails resting in her lap. She hadn't had to think about that night for months. She looked Lori in the eyes. "All right, I'll tell you about it. My boyfriend, Sam, was in jail for a few weeks. After he got out, he found me. We went back to where I was sleeping, and everything was fine ... until these two guys busted in on us." Rose stopped to take a deep breath, then continued. "One sells drugs, the other is an enforcer. Everyone knows them as Moss and Shep."

"Then what happened?"

"They had a beef with Sam. I don't know what Sam did to get them so upset because he didn't do drugs. All I could figure was maybe he sold some and didn't hand over the money he owed them. I don't know. See, he didn't tell me everything and I didn't ask questions." Her emotions were getting the better of her, so she stopped to collect herself, and then resumed. "Shep pulled a knife. I didn't want any part of that, so I tried to get out of their way. Somewhere along, I got pushed so hard that I lost one of my shoes. I think it was Sam who pushed me. Then I ran the best I could 'cause I only had one shoe. I hobbled over to a dumpster across the street with one bare foot and hid, but I knew they saw where I went. I kept looking to see what happened. I wish I hadn't. It was gross. Shep's elbow kept repeatedly jutting out from the side of the partition beside the door. He was stabbing Sam. Over and over."

Rose's eyes filled with tears, but she continued. "Then Moss pulled out a garbage bag, like the one I used to carry around, and they stuffed Sam in the bag. Then both men dragged off the bag. I don't know where they went."

Lori was silent for a minute, digesting what she just heard. "So, they know you saw them murder Sam, your boyfriend?"

"Yes, for sure. When they left, Moss looked over at me hiding behind the dumpster. I guess I wasn't hidden very well. He pointed right at me, then did a motion with his finger across his neck. I knew he was sending a message that he'd slice my throat if I told."

"So, you can identify these men?"

"Yes. I saw them the next day, and that same guy took his finger and ran it across his neck again. I got the message. I was scared, so I came here ... eventually," Rose said, biting her lower lip.

Lori sighed softly. "You should have told me this earlier. What if one of those two men had come in here? I think you are in danger, Rose."

"I was afraid of that. I guess I thought the longer this goes on, they'll forget about me, maybe think I left town."

"We should call the police." Lori picked up the receiver to her office phone.

"No! Don't call! I won't testify against them," she said, fear radiating from her body. "I'll leave, go somewhere else."

Lori put the phone back in the cradle. "Rose, you need to make a charge against these men so they can't kill anyone else."

"Maybe so, but I won't do it."

"If one of them were to come in here, you could be in danger," she said quietly.

"I'll take my chances. I'm not telling. No way."

The expression on Rose's face was so intense, Lori couldn't argue further. "If you insist, Rose.

Afterwards, Rose slinked back to her bed, feeling like she was dragging chains. She could almost hear the past scraping along. She lay on the cot, closed her eyes, and remembered a few weeks back. She had walked into the dining hall for dinner. Three new men were seated at a table. One of them was Shep, one of the men she had just been talking about with Lori. She quickly slipped out before he saw her.

In fear, she had gone without dinner that night. In the morning, she returned to the dining hall and was relieved to see he was not there. She hadn't seen him again at the shelter. Rose prayed silently that he never returned and left town—and left her in peace.

TWENTY-EIGHT

ABBY HAD JUST SETTLED into the couch to watch TV. Seely was curled up beside her, purring like crazy. Both were content after a long day at work and guarding the apartment. Then a loud knock came from the door. Actually, it sounded more like a booming, the knock was so forceful. Abby crossed to the door and peeked out the peephole to see who it was. *Eric! Again!*

She flung open the door in anger. "What do you want?" she asked loudly.

"Just you. Only you," Eric slurred, then gave her a lopsided smile.

"I'm not interested. Leave," she said, blocking his entrance with her body. He wasn't coming in this time.

"Aw, honeybun. It's me, your adorable husband."

"I am not arguing with you, Eric. Please leave or I'll call the police."

Abby stood firmly between the door and the jamb, but Eric tried to push through. "Stop! You can't come in! Eric, get back!" She shuffled against him, trying to prevent his entry. "You're drunk; get away from me. I mean it."

HAIRCUT AND HIGHLIGHTS

Abby heard her neighbor's door open and footsteps approach. It was Mark to the rescue.

"Hey, mister, get back from the lady's door," he ordered, jolting Eric to attention.

Eric turned to face Mark, looking confused. "Who are you?" he snarled.

"No one you want to mess with. I suggest you leave now, while you're able," Mark said, frowning at the intruder.

"Yeah? Who says?" Eric swayed backwards in his defiance. "You ain't nobody."

Mark smiled, showing perfect, white teeth. "I'm about to be somebody to you: the guy who throws you down a flight of stairs."

"What?" Eric made a raspberry sound.

"Okay, fella, enough of your crap." He grabbed Eric by the arm and shoulders and propelled him forward to the head of the staircase.

Eric resisted all the way until he stood at the top, looking down at the expanse of stairs.

"One choice: leave or be tossed down."

Eric swung his head around and looked up with his mouth open. Mark was glaring at him. "I'll go," he said, taking the first step after Mark released his hold on him. But then he stumbled and had to move his legs as fast as he could to keep from falling. He reached for the railing to keep from tumbling all the way down. Eric glanced back at Mark, then walked down the rest of the steps, feigning dignity, and left the building.

Mark returned to Abby. "Who was that?"

"I'm sorry to say my ex-husband."

"That makes sense. Are you all right?"

She could see the concern in his eyes. "Yes, I'm fine," she replied, suddenly realizing she was standing in the hall dressed in her nightgown and bathrobe. "Thank you for coming to my rescue."

"Hey, it's my job," he said with a grin. "If he comes back again, don't hesitate to call for me. I'll come running."

"I'll definitely do that." Abby gave him a big smile, then went inside her apartment.

"Oh, Seely, you wouldn't believe what happened." She crossed back to the couch and flounced into it.

Abby resumed watching the program but was distracted. Why had Eric come by? Was he visiting his parents again, or had he made a special trip to harass her? It was hard to know the answer. With Eric, anything was possible. His brain didn't function like that of normal people. But what could she expect from an alcoholic?

She felt fortunate that Mark had heard them arguing in the hall. Fortunate he was home to send Eric on his way, even if that could have meant him being thrown bodily down the stairs. If he showed up again, she would not open the door. Let him think she wasn't home. But Abby thought he wouldn't return. Not after his encounter with Mark, her protector. After all, he wasn't a total idiot.

Ivy was very uncomfortable as she attempted to set a woman's hair. Abby was concerned. "How do you feel?" she asked as Ivy wound a large strand of hair over a roller.

"Like I ate an elephant's leg, followed by the tusk for dessert."

Abby looked at the young woman, her heart going out to her. Ivy was coming close to her term, but it was a bit early for the delivery. Yet it sounded like her body was signaling that the baby wanted out, sooner than planned. "Do you have a bag packed?"

"Yes. And Mrs. York is all set to move into action." Ivy wound the last strand of hair around the roller.

Mrs. York was a peach. Her grandmotherly instincts were

HAIRCUT AND HIGHLIGHTS

kicking in, preparing to assume that duty even though the baby wasn't related to her. Abby knew Ivy was fortunate to have Mrs. York in her life. "So, Mrs. York is taking you to the hospital?"

"Yes, unless it happens here, and you'll take me, right?" she asked as she walked her client to the dryers.

"Of course, I will. I'd be delighted."

"Then everything is in order. And Mrs. York will bring the bag to the hospital." Ivy's face radiated pleasure at having her delivery planned out.

"Are you scared?" Abby asked.

"I'm not talking about that. Trying not to think about the delivery." Ivy waddled back to her chair to sit, placing her hand over the swollen belly. "But I want an epidural, that's for sure."

Abby grinned. *I would, too.*

Sonia came in from lunch, walking quickly to her chair. "Whew! My boyfriend so silly," she said, looking into the mirror to straighten her hair.

Abby wondered what kind of lunch break Sonia had taken.

When Sonia turned from the mirror, her eyes fell on Ivy. "Ah, you close, right?"

Ivy's eyes widened. "Not *that* close."

"Ah, I think yes. You be little mama soon." Sonia smiled as she wiped down her chair and counter. "Little mama. Bambino coming soon," she sang.

Ivy threw a scared expression at Abby. She was clearly unnerved by the comments.

"We'll just have to wait and see what the baby decides." She gave Ivy an encouraging smile. "Everything will be fine."

However, Abby secretly agreed with Sonia. From the looks of Ivy's significantly dropped baby bump, and the way she was acting, Abby felt the baby could come any time. Even that afternoon.

And she was right in her assessment. At about three o'clock, Ivy doubled over in pain and let out an agonized holler. When she stood straight again, her eyes were bugged out. "Ah-hh, that was awful. Was that a contraction?"

"I think so, sweetie," Abby said.

"Ooh, I tell you, *today*." Sonia looked over at the young woman and pointed a rattail comb at her. "Bambino coming."

"You'd better sit in your chair," Abby advised.

The girl didn't need encouragement to do that. She quickly fell into the chair, breathing heavily.

Abby looked over at Sonia. "You've had babies, I haven't. What should we do?"

"Count from one contraction to next. She start at three," Sonia said with authority.

"Would you like some water?" Abby asked.

"Yes," Ivy said, rubbing her belly.

Abby went to the back and retrieved a bottle of water, bringing it back to Ivy. Ivy drank and relaxed until the next contraction ten minutes later. She let out a long groan, squinted, and closed her eyes. Another groan followed quickly.

Abby looked at the clock on the wall. Three-ten. Her eyes shot over to Sonia.

"Time for hospital," was all Sonia said.

"Okay, we need to get you to the hospital." Abby took Ivy's arm to help her up.

"Will I fit in your car?"

There was a thought. Abby's car was tiny. How comfortable could she be in that vehicle? "I hadn't thought about that."

Ivy groaned again, but softer. "Get Aunt Bobbi. She has a big car."

"I'll be right back." Abby ran next door.

TWENTY-NINE

BOBBI WAS STOPPED at a light on the way to Halifax Hospital. Abby was riding shotgun, with Ivy in the backseat. Ivy was the only one not strapped in, due to the size of her belly and wanting to lie down across the seat.

"We aren't far now," Bobbi said. "Another five minutes and we'll pull into the emergency room." She glanced to the back at her niece. "It's okay, honey. Almost there. Five minutes."

Ivy let out another loud groan, followed by a growl. Bobbi moved the car forward when the light changed. Then the unexpected happened. A guy in a pickup truck didn't stop for the red light. Bobbi saw him coming but couldn't avoid him. He plowed into the driver's side of the car, pushing the vehicle completely out of his path, so it faced south instead of west. Ivy screamed from the backseat. No one knew if from her contractions or an injury. When the car came to a stop, Abby was the first to speak.

"I'm okay," she shouted, noticing her bleeding right arm. Looking at Bobbi, she asked if she was okay.

Bobbi was leaning over the console, her arms touching Abby's legs. "I don't know. It's hard to move," was her breathless reply. "Ivy? Are you okay?" she mumbled, unable to turn toward her.

"No!" Her shrill response alarmed both women.

Abby unfastened her seatbelt and looked to the backseat. Ivy was sprawled on the floor, wedged between the seats. "Honey, does anything hurt?"

"My leg! It's under the front seat."

Abby saw that Bobbi's seat was crushed under the door, probably trapping Ivy's leg.

"An ambulance will be here soon. We're just around the corner from the hospital, honey. Hang on. Help is coming," Abby told her, trying to retain her composure and sound encouraging. Now was not the time to get hysterical, no matter how shook up she felt.

An old man rapped on her broken window. Abby released the handle so the door fell open.

"I called 911. They'll be here in a jiffy," said the man. "Are you all okay?"

"We have a pregnant woman in the back and my friend is hurt," Abby answered.

A siren interrupted the conversation, the patrol vehicle pulling close to the car. Two police officers stepped out.

"Ma'am? Are you all right?" someone asked. "Abby!"

She looked up—into Jack's face.

"Let me help you out," he said, reaching toward her.

"I'm okay, but Bobbi's hurt, and Ivy in the back is pregnant and in labor. Tend to her first," Abby ordered. "Why are you here? You're not patrol," she said, noticing his hair had grown back as she stepped out.

"I was in my car across the street. I saw everything happen, so I'm here to assist."

"Oh."

Another police vehicle arrived, along with a fire truck and ambulance. After that, Abby lost track of the vehicles and Jack.

HAIRCUT AND HIGHLIGHTS

Someone else had assisted Abby to the ambulance while numerous men determined what the situation was inside the vehicle. She watched them attempt to open the driver's side door, which wouldn't budge.

Official looking people leaned into the vehicle from the opposite side to help Ivy, who appeared to be stuck. Somehow, they managed to pull Bobbi from the passenger side, and placed her on a stretcher. Two firemen entered the car from the back and front, ripping out the driver's seat. Once that was accomplished, they removed Ivy and placed her on a stretcher, and quickly transported her to the hospital. Another ambulance took Bobbi away while Abby's arm was being wrapped in the first ambulance that had arrived. Eventually, she was taken to the emergency room.

Abby's injury was stitched and wrapped in gauze. Otherwise, except for being shaken, she was fine. When she was finished being cared for, she called Mrs. York from a waiting room.

"No, I don't know anything yet. But you should bring the bag for Ivy. She's not going anywhere soon." Abby told her where she was waiting so they could meet. She thought about making other calls, then realized the staff would contact the necessary family members.

"Abby, are you all right?" a male voice asked. She looked up to see Mark in uniform.

"Mark!" she said, smiling gently. "Were you there?"

"Yes. In the firetruck." He sat beside her. "Your arm?"

"The window cut me. Just a few stitches, and I'll be fine. No big deal," she said, even though it hurt like the dickens. She appreciated the company, though. "What about the others?"

"They're examining the driver. I think she'll be okay. I don't really know much, though."

"And Ivy? The pregnant one?"

"There was damage to her ankle or foot when we pulled her

out. I think they patched her up quickly so they could get her into delivery. I don't know more than that."

He had the kindest eyes Abby had ever seen: gentle blue, with a darker surrounding rim of blue. His eyebrows were heavy. Such a handsome man.

"Do you need a ride home?" he asked.

"I don't think so. I really want to know how everyone is, and someone is bringing Ivy some clothes, so I can always ride back with her." Abby looked into his clean-shaven face and neatly clipped hair. "But thank you for asking."

A nurse came out and looked at Abby. "Are you with the ladies in the accident? One is pregnant."

"Yes, that's me. How are they?"

"The driver has some trauma, so we want to observe her overnight, given her age. She has a few broken ribs, but we don't think she has any internal injuries. She should be fine."

"And the pregnant one, Ivy?"

"Her foot was somewhat damaged, given it was pinned under the front seat. Mostly lacerations and bruising. She's in delivery right now, waiting for the arrival of her baby. Just a matter of time," she said with a quick smile. "We hope nothing happened to the baby when she was thrown on the floor. I'll keep you posted."

"Thank you; I appreciate that. She's an employee, but I'm very fond of her, like she's my little sister."

"I understand," she said, then turned to leave.

"She'll be fine. Don't worry," Mark said.

"I'm trying not to. I've been praying."

"That always helps."

"You really believe that?"

"Yes, I do. Really."

He smiled at her with sincerity.

She couldn't believe what she was hearing. "Are you a man of faith?"

"Yes."

"You are a rare breed," she said, her respect for him growing. "How could I run into a burning building and not be?"

"I can't imagine." She smiled into his face.

Several hours later, Abby brought two coffees into the waiting area, handing one to Mrs. York.

"While you were gone, someone came in and said Ivy was giving birth," she said, accepting the coffee.

"Then we'll know soon if she really has a girl." Abby smiled at the older woman as she sat beside her. "Sometimes, they get it wrong."

"I'm betting on a boy," Mr. Banworthy said. "At least, I hope it's a boy. Much easier to raise."

Bobbi's husband had come to see his wife, and then came into the waiting room to give a report. Bobbi would be fine, and could go home the next day, providing nothing occurred overnight to delay her release.

"Men always want boys," Mrs. York said. "But she's going to have a sweet little girl."

"Women always want girls," he responded.

She shot him a stern look from across the room.

The door separating the waiting room from the behind-the-scenes activity in the hospital swung open. A man who looked like a doctor swept through the opening, removing his mask. He was brief and to the point. "It's a girl."

Everyone hooped and hollered with joy.

"What are her stats?" Mrs. York asked.

"Six and a half pounds, nineteen inches, and a head full of black hair," he said evenly, like he gave that sort of information daily, which he probably did. "Baby and mother are just fine, no problems."

"I wonder what she'll name her," Mr. Banworthy mused aloud.

"I haven't heard her mention anything about a name," Abby said.

"You can see her in about an hour," the doctor said as he turned to leave. He swept back through the doors before they closed behind him.

Later, a woman entered through another door. She looked harried and slightly disheveled. Abby thought the woman had hastily thrown on some clothes. "If you're waiting to see Ivy, we are, too."

She turned to look at Abby, pointing at her. "Are you the one who's her boss?"

"Yes, I am. My name is Abby Bugsly."

"I'm Ivy's mother, Helen," she stated and then said to Mr. Banworthy, "Hello, Frank."

Her brother nodded at her but didn't speak.

"How is my sister-in-law?" she asked him.

"She'll be fine. A few broken ribs, shook up, but doing okay." He looked disapprovingly at his sister. "She'll go home tomorrow. Don't you want to know about your daughter?"

"Of course. Did she have the baby? I didn't even know she was pregnant," Helen said, extending her hands upward.

"It's a little girl," Abby said.

"What's the name?"

"We don't know yet. We're waiting to see her," Mrs. York said.

"And who are you?" Helen asked.

"Her landlady and soon-to-be nanny. You can call me Mrs. York."

"I can help with the baby, too," Helen said as she walked toward a chair. "I know Ivy will need help with the baby. She doesn't know anything about kids."

"I would suggest you discuss that issue with Ivy," Mrs. York said stiffly.

"Well, I *am* the grandmother," Helen declared, as if suggesting the title gave her some rights.

Mrs. York let the conversation drop. That was a discussion best had between daughter and mother.

Abby looked at her watch before she spoke. "It's been an hour. Let's go visit Ivy and meet the baby."

THIRTY

IVY WAS LYING in bed with her baby hugged close. Her auburn hair was fanned out over the pillow like a pinwheel. She looked tired, but happy.

"Ivy! Your baby!" Abby cried as she walked into the room. "How are you feeling?"

Ivy looked at her through tired eyes and had a wan smile on her face. "Better now. I'm tired."

"Of course, you are, child," Mrs. York said, bustling to the side of the bed. "Oh, such a beautiful face!" She pulled the blanket back from the baby's head for a better view.

"My grandchild," Helen said, coming to the other side of the bed.

Ivy immediately tensed and looked afraid, tightening her arms around the baby. "Mama! What are you doing here?"

"They called me. I'm your mother, the next of kin." Helen smiled at her daughter, looking from her face to the baby's and back.

Ivy shook her head. "No, no, no. I don't want you here." Her eyes grew large and she looked to Mrs. York for help. "Get her out of here."

"But Ivy, I'm your mother. I have a right to be here."

"Maybe another time? When Ivy is rested," Abby suggested, coming to Helen's side. "She's been through a lot in one day. The accident, giving birth. She needs some time."

Helen looked from Abby to Ivy. "Well, okay. I'll go for now, but I'll be back." She left the room.

Tears welled in Ivy's eyes. "Why does she have to ruin everything?"

"She's gone, Ivy. It's okay," Mrs. York said softly.

"I'll stand guard so she can't return," said Frank, still standing at the door.

"Uncle Frank. Nice to see you," Ivy smiled. "How is Aunt Bobbi?"

"She's in another room, recovering. She'll be fine." He walked closer. "Probably get out tomorrow."

Ivy looked at Abby, now standing beside the bed. "Are you okay?"

"I'm fine. Just a little scratch," she said, pointing to her arm. "No big deal."

"That's good. My foot is bandaged up." Ivy stuck her right leg outside the covers to show them. "Nothing serious."

"Have you decided on a name yet?" Mrs. York asked.

Ivy's face brightened into a big smile. "Yes, I have. Her name is Luna Jane."

"Luna?" Mrs. York asked.

"It means moon. She's named after the moon goddess," Ivy answered, adjusting the baby's blanket closer. "Luna. Isn't that pretty? And Jane is my middle name."

"Very nice, Ivy," Abby said, sensing Mrs. York thought the name was strange.

"Good choice, Ivy," Frank smiled. "I'll tell your aunt."

"I'll leave your bag on this chair, Ivy." Mrs. York plunked down the satchel on the chair. "It should get you by until you're released."

"Thank you."

"Now, I best leave and let you rest after your ordeal," Mrs. York said.

"Oh, that means me, too. She's my ride," Abby said with a smile. She leaned in close to Ivy and gave her a kiss on the cheek.

Mrs. York did the same. "Let me know when to pick you up," she said. "And I'll begin the final preparations at home for the arrival of Luna."

Ivy giggled. "My baby. Luna."

And the baby cooed right on cue.

———

The women climbed into Mrs. York's large Buick, certainly roomy enough for Ivy and the baby.

"Poor Bobbi. Her car is totaled." Abby clicked her seatbelt closed.

"I hope the other guy has insurance." Mrs. York started the engine.

"Me, too."

"What is your opinion about Helen seeing her grandchild?" asked Mrs. York as she pulled away from the parking lot.

"That is Ivy's decision."

"But shouldn't she let her see the child?"

"Ivy is afraid of her mother. She thinks she'll beat on the baby like she beat on her," Abby said, watching as they passed under the traffic light.

"A baby? Oh, never." Mrs. York was clearly horrified at such an idea.

"You never know with people. Some just aren't kind. And others are messed up, so you can't trust them around children." She shook her head.

"I suppose. I just know I'd be devastated if I couldn't see my grandchild," Mrs. York said, carefully going through another intersection.

"We have to respect Ivy's wishes."

"I know you're right."

"Do you need any help with the new baby preparations? I'm perfectly willing to come over and pitch in," Abby offered.

"Nothing much needs to be done. Maybe stack up some diapers around the changing table, put the wipes there, things like that. Most everything is done."

"Sounds like you can handle all that," Abby said, not wanting to take away any duties Mrs. York was looking forward to doing. "But if you need me, just call."

"I will, dear." She pulled around the corner onto Beach Street.

Abby saw some homeless people milling around. They reminded her that she hadn't seen Rose in months. The thought saddened her that she may never see Rose again, even if she was alive.

Mrs. York stopped in front of the salon.

"Thank you for the ride home."

"My pleasure, dear," she said with a smile.

Abby started to get out but stopped when she saw that same homeless man who had been hanging around her salon. He was peering into the salon again.

"Hey, you," she called out the window. "What are you doing here?"

The man, looking no cleaner than before, shot her a shocked expression. He turned immediately and ran like a jackrabbit.

"I can't believe he came back!" Abby said shakily.

"Who was that?"

"A homeless guy. I suspect he had something to do with the murder on my doorstep. He keeps coming here."

"You should call the police," Mrs. York advised her, concern written on her face. "He could be dangerous."

"You're right, and I will," Abby said, getting out of the car. "Goodbye, Mrs. York. We'll talk soon."

After closing the car door, she sprinted to the downstairs door of the building, unlocked it, and quickly climbed the stairs to her apartment. Once inside, she leaned her back on the door, sliding to the floor where she remained until she had finished a good cry.

Seely joined her mid-cry, purring and curling up with her. "Seely," she said, stroking the cat. "I'm so glad to be home. Poor Bobbi. Her car is ruined."

Thoughts of the accident she'd experienced with her parents came flooding in. The terror, the fear, the emotional pain. She could almost smell the burning rubber. It was difficult to put that scene out of her mind. Dreams had haunted her for years after, and this recent accident had added to the trauma. She forced herself to think about something else.

"Ivy finally had her baby," she said, a smile tugging at her downturned lips. "She wasn't hurt much in the accident. And then her mother came. Uh, too much to think about. I'm exhausted. Let's go to bed, huh?"

Abby pulled herself off the floor, wincing when she put pressure on her arm. "Darn stitches."

She went to her bedroom to change. When she returned from the bathroom, she said prayers of gratitude and snuggled in with her kitty, careful to keep the kitten away from her sore arm. Seely's comforting purrs reverberated through her body most of the night, lulling her to sleep.

Rose Tumbler followed Grace Davenport upstairs and down a long hallway to the end bedroom. Along the way, she passed two bathrooms. Grace was the supervisor of the halfway house. A kindly woman who had a soft spot for women in trouble.

"That bed is yours," Grace said, pointing at the one on the right. "The other belongs to your roommate. I hope you don't mind sharing. We have limited space and she said she didn't mind. We thought you'd prefer to be with her."

"This will be fine," Rose said, placing her suitcase on the bed. "Thank you for taking me in." She had just come from a dormitory, so sharing a room with one person during her time in transitional housing was a pleasant change. As long as the roommate didn't snore.

"You're welcome, Rose." Grace shut the door as she left.

While Rose unpacked, the new roommate came into their bedroom.

"Hey. I heard I was getting someone," she said, sitting on the edge of her bed. "I'm Patti Miracle."

"Miracle? That's a beautiful name."

"Yeah, my life's a miracle. A miracle I'm still alive," she said with a laugh.

"I'm Rose Tumbler. I've tumbled around a lot in my life," she laughed. "How long have you been here?"

"Couple months. I have a job now and I'm saving to move into my own place."

Rose noticed a scar beside Patti's right eye, shaped in an arc. Several decorated her bare arms, and another long scar appeared to run down her thigh from underneath her shorts. *It probably is a miracle she's alive.*

"I'm homeless. Er, that's not true. I *was* homeless. I'm trying really hard to get back to normal living," Rose said, shaking the wrinkles out of a denim shirt.

"Yeah, me, too. Still am till I move out," Patti said. "But for now, this is my home. So, welcome home."

"Thanks. Do you like being here?"

"Yes and no. I like not being on the street. So far, I like my new job. But I'm anxious to live on my own." She pulled her long brown hair into a scrunchie.

"Where do you work?"

"I'm in training for restaurant management," Patti replied, fidgeting with her fingers, then chewing a fingernail. "I'll be the assistant after training, but it's a chain restaurant, so I can move up if I go to another place when there's an opening."

"That sounds promising."

"Yeah. I have a future instead of being on the street with nothing good happening, ever."

"I have an interview for an office job," Rose said.

"That's good."

"When I leave here, I plan to see a woman who was trying to help me. She'll be surprised. I hope when she sees the change in me, she'll let me stay with her for a while. She's really nice," Rose said, closing her suitcase.

"Good luck with that. People don't like the homeless."

"She's different. A real Christian lady. I know she'll help me out." Rose looked longingly out at nothing, remembering Abby's kindness.

"I gotta go. My turn to help with dinner." Patti rose from the bed. "Good experience for my job. See ya down there."

"I'll be there." *Patti seems okay. I could do worse for a roommate.*

THIRTY-ONE

AFTER LUNCH THE NEXT DAY, Rose walked down the hallway to her assigned bedroom. The counseling session had gone well that morning, leaving her to feel she could pass the interview for a job. The longer she was in this program, the more she wanted to get on with her life. Being a normal human being, a woman with a job, apartment, and car was becoming highly appealing. She could live like everyone else. There was a time when she had.

She kicked off her shoes and lay down, thinking she'd take a nap, but her thoughts got in the way. The memory of her father interrupted any flow to sleep. *The bastard.* She could have called him much worse. He had never had a kind word for her, only criticism. As far as he was concerned, she was worthless. Now, if she'd been a boy, that would have been a completely different story. No doubt he would have praised a son, his mirror image ... but only in his mind. Her father, she came to understand, was the reason she hadn't bounced back after she lost her job and apartment, and then the car. She felt, at the time, she hadn't deserved anything better than being on the street. After all, she was worthless. He had told her so. Being homeless confirmed his previous opinion.

After a few months of counseling, Rose's opinion of herself had changed radically and her self-esteem had grown significantly. It was like a light bulb turned on in her brain. No longer did Rose view herself as worthless or deserving to be homeless. *No one* deserved to be without a roof over her head or a job. Rose was now able to see herself as worthy of good things. Finally. She was not going to allow her father to control her thoughts or actions anymore. He had not earned any rights in her life. How could she continue to permit him entry, even if it was only through her thinking? She didn't even know if he was alive. Most likely, he was deceased due to his drinking. She *must* consider him dead to her.

"Dead," she said aloud, and closed her eyes. Sleep quickly took her.

Goldilocks was so busy, Abby thought it must be New Year's Eve, but it wasn't. It seemed every client each operator had acquired was present at one time. Even after taking four weeks maternity leave, Ivy was surfing from one client to the next as fast as her legs would take her. She had thought she'd lose some clients, but they waited for her return, which pleased her.

"So, tell me all about Luna," requested Miriam. She was a steady client and had brought a baby gift with her, much to Ivy's joy.

Ivy had been regaling all her clients with stories about Luna's feeding and sleeping habits, so she unleashed her storehouse of tales on Miriam.

"And where is your precious baby?"

"Mrs. York, my landlady, is watching her right now. She

volunteered to help since she doesn't have anything much to do," Ivy replied while towel drying Miriam's hair.

"That was very understanding and caring of your needs," Miriam said. "You are so fortunate."

"Don't I know it." Ivy twisted rollers into Miriam's damp hair. "She loves Luna so much, and never complains about anything to do with caring for her."

"She's a saint. Child-care can be tough. I raised six kids. Four were boys. Not an easy thing to do."

"Four boys? Um, no thank you." Ivy wrapped another swath of hair around a roller. "One little girl is enough for me."

"Do you hear from the daddy?" she asked.

"Nope, and I don't expect to. He doesn't know about Luna," Ivy said, hoping Miriam didn't push for information.

"You should tell him, Ivy. He has a right to know."

"He'd think I wanted him to pay child support."

"You could use the income, couldn't you?" she asked.

"Yes, it would be nice. But I'm not sure he's in town anymore," Ivy replied, reaching for more rollers.

"I think you should check that out," Miriam suggested in a soft tone.

"Maybe. I don't know." Ivy had thought about locating George, but that was as far as any action had gone. He'd probably be freaked if she told him he got her pregnant. Scott sure was when she thought it was his baby. This was an uncomfortable situation to be in. She couldn't imagine George relishing the idea of paying child support. However, he did rightfully owe that support. She was entitled to ask. And Miriam was correct, George should be told; he had a right to know he was a father.

"Think about talking to him, Ivy." Miriam smiled kindly at her.

"I will."

The bell jingled and Miriam's eyes suddenly opened wide as she stared over Ivy's shoulder. Ivy turned her head to see who had entered, then gasped. A large scruffy man stood at the door. His scraggly hair stuck out from under a knitted cap, and his beard looked like someone had hacked at it with a knife in an attempt to shorten it, then stopped halfway through.

Abby also turned from where she was standing behind a customer to see who had come into the salon. She dropped the brush she was holding, taking a step backwards out of fear. *It's him!* She couldn't believe the man she had seen peering into her salon was now standing six feet away. *Inside!* Every instinct screamed that the man was trouble. Normally, she had compassion for the homeless, but not for him.

"Sir, you need to leave," she said after mustering courage. "Right now."

The man's eyes glared between the strands of greasy hair that fell in his face. He didn't speak, probably knowing she'd call the police. Slowly, he turned around, taking in every detail of the salon. After grabbing the doorknob, he pulled open the door and spit on the glass before leaving. The door slammed shut behind him.

Trembling, Abby quickly ran to the door and turned the deadbolt. When she turned around, everyone in the salon was staring at her.

"I-I don't know w-what just happened. I-I am at a loss for words," she stammered, walking back to her station, picking up the dropped brush.

"Homeless, I tell you," said Sonia, shaking her head.

"Probably on drugs," stated Miriam.

Ivy just stood, wide-eyed, looking at Abby.

"Your friend, Rose? Mm, he come because of her," Sonia said. "Bad actor."

"Yes, he is, Sonia." Abby's thoughts chased an explanation. His returning had to mean he was involved in the stabbing of the other man. He wasn't coming back to get a haircut; he was checking out the place, possibly looking for Rose. That would make sense if he were responsible for the bloodshed at her doorstep ... where Rose once slept. *Or was he looking for Rose because he knew she saw something?*

Abby walked to the supply room. After rooting around for a few minutes, she found a small empty bottle that had been cleaned. With the bottle in hand, she went to the door and attempted to gather some of the spittle adhered to it in the bottle.

"I don't think it takes much," she said as everyone in the room watched. "I think I got a decent amount, though."

Abby closed the door and bolted it again. She pulled out her cell and punched in the number for Jack. After he answered, she told him about the homeless man's visits and the spit she had collected.

"I'll be right over for the bottle," he said. "That will help a lot. Good work, Abby."

"Thanks. I thought I should let the professionals handle it from here," she said with a chuckle.

"Okay, I deserve that." Jack clicked off the phone.

―――

Rose was nervous as she entered a building associated with an internationally known telephone company. Everything around her appeared larger than life, with the bright white walls and ceilings surrounding an equally bright white tiled floor. The entry was pristine, as was the huge reception area that followed. She walked to the desk to inquire about where the employment office was located.

"Take one of those elevators behind me to the third floor. When you exit, turn right to the first set of double doors. There's a sign saying Human Resources. You can't miss it," the woman said in a deep southern accent. She was dressed nicely, making Rose wonder if her outfit was suitable for the interview. It had been provided by kind donors to the shelter.

Once on the third floor, she saw more white walls, ceilings, and tiled floors. The inside of the office for Human Resources was no different.

"I'm Rose Tumbler," she said to a receptionist behind the desk. "I have an appointment with Mrs. Minton."

"Yes, she's expecting you. Let me buzz her." The woman touched an intercom button and spoke when the person on the other end answered. "Rose Tumbler is here." Looking up at Rose, she said, "She'll be right out."

Mrs. Minton appeared in the doorway, a tall woman with graying hair. "Rose, so nice to see you. Please follow me."

Rose silently followed the older woman into an office just off the narrow hallway.

"Please have a seat."

She selected one of the three chairs across from the woman behind the desk. Feeling more nervous than she had in years, Rose tried her best to wear a calm expression.

"Your application shows you have a clerical background and computer knowledge. Is that right?"

"Yes, ma'am."

"Good, good. We need women like you," she said, smiling. Her face was gently lined, appearing kind. "I understand you are rebuilding your life."

"Yes, I am trying to do that."

"I'm sure it's an adjustment for you. But I have to commend you for your effort," she said. "Not everyone has the moxie to pull themselves up when they've been down."

"All I can do is try."

"Yes, dear. Try. If you don't do that, you won't go anywhere, right?"

"Yes, ma'am."

"Okay, we have several openings, and I don't see any reason

one of them couldn't be yours." Mrs. Minton handed Rose a sheet of paper with a job description printed on it. "Please read that and see if it suits you."

Rose read the details of the clerical position. She didn't see anything she wasn't capable of doing, and nothing was distasteful. She used to like dealing with the public, until she had reason to be afraid of people. Handling a receptionist's phone wasn't difficult; she had done that task for years. Researching on the computer wasn't hard, and certainly typing memos, drafts and creating projects on Excel was familiar. This was a job she could accomplish with no problem.

"I can do all of this. I *did* all of this at one time. The job sounds like something I would enjoy." Rose handed the sheet back to Mrs. Minton.

"So, Rose, are you accepting our job offer?" she asked with a little smile.

"Yes, ma'am," Rose answered, wearing a large smile. "I happily accept."

"Good, good. Can you start on Monday?"

"Yes, ma'am." The butterflies were calming down, but her excitement was building.

Mrs. Minton stood and extended a hand to Rose. "Welcome, dear."

"Thank you."

"Just report to this office on Monday, and I'll show you where you will be working."

"Yes, ma'am."

Rose had to refrain from skipping out of the office, her excitement was so great. Once back in the elevator, she let out a whoop and holler. "I did it!"

Abby was going to be so surprised and proud of her.

THIRTY-TWO

IVY SENT out a few texts to friends, asking where George was. Two people told her he worked at a company that built boats and yachts. She knew where the place was located and decided to pay him a visit there.

Mrs. York took care of the baby while she attempted to see George. Guessing what time he got off work, she hung out in the parking lot. A half hour later, she was pleased to see George approaching his car. She was parked next to it.

"Hey, George!" she called, getting out of the car she'd borrowed from Mrs. York.

"Ivy?" he asked, looking surprised to see her. "I can't believe it's you." George looked tanned and buff under his tee. His hair was sun-bleached to a soft blonde; even his eyebrows were.

"Hi, George," she said, looking up into his face. "You look great."

"So do you, girl. Hot," he said with a smile.

"Thanks."

"Why are you here?"

"Can we go somewhere and talk?"

"Sure. Want to catch a beer at Polo's?"

"Okay."

They both got into their own cars and drove to a small bar near Beach Street. When they entered, George found them a quiet table on the side. They placed their order for two drafts.

"I guess you know I work at the yacht building place," he said.

"So I was told."

"It's good work, perfect for me because I love to build things, work with my hands. Love the creative side, too. And it pays good." He smiled broadly at Ivy, like he thought he was impressing her.

The server returned with two mugs of beer.

"That's great, George. I work as a hairdresser at Goldilocks on Beach," she said with a smile. "I love what I do. The pay varies from week to week, plus I'm still building a clientele."

"I remember you were going to school for that. I'm glad you got hooked up to a salon and you like your job. What about your mom?"

"Yeah, about that. I moved out. I rent a room in a house that a sweet old lady owns near the salon. I couldn't deal with my mother anymore. She didn't improve with age." Ivy rolled her eyes, then gave him a half-hearted smile.

"Still pushed you around, huh?"

"More like punched me around."

"Ow. I'm sorry. You don't deserve that."

"No, I don't. I don't have anything to do with her, even though I have a …" Ivy stopped short from saying "baby". "Whatever, she's not in my life."

"So, what have you been doing?" he asked, taking a taste of his beer.

"Well, that's why I wanted to talk to you," she said, hesitating.

"What? What's up?" His smile crinkled his eyes.

"I had a baby recently. A little girl. Her name is Luna," Ivy replied, not able to contain her smile.

"Wow, that's great, Ivy. Congratulations." George looked genuinely pleased for her.

"I have some pictures here." She reached into her purse and handed some to George.

"Ah, Ivy, she's adorable," he said, all smiles as he looked at the pictures. "What a lucky girl she is to have you as a mommy."

"Thanks. She also has you as a daddy."

George rotated his head toward her and stared in silence. His mouth opened, but nothing came out for a few seconds. "Daddy? I'm a *daddy?*" he finally squeaked out.

"Yup. You the daddy."

"I'm ... stunned. Shocked. I don't know what to say."

"Let it sink in for a minute," she said, nodding. "You can imagine my surprise when I found out. Oh, and you can have those pictures. They're duplicates."

"I like this one, the two of you," he said, pointing at the picture on the table. "She looks like you."

"And you. Look at that nose and her lips."

"Yeah, I see it." George stopped looking at the pictures and looked at Ivy. "So, I guess you'd like some money?"

"That would be nice, but that's not the main reason I'm here."

"Then *why* are you here?"

"You have a right to know you have a child. I couldn't keep this from you. You deserve to know you fathered a child," she explained, looking at him squarely. "It's just that simple."

"You're right about that. And I'm glad you told me," he said. "I can't believe I'm a father."

"I can't believe I'm a mother. I'm only twenty." She sat back heavily against the chair.

"Yeah, this has to be quite an adjustment for you."

"You have no idea."

"Ivy, this may come as a surprise to you, but I'm really happy about this," he said. The expression of sincerity on his face made

Ivy believe what he said was true. "Luna is beautiful and I love kids. Ivy, we are *parents*!"

Ivy laughed. This was not the reaction she'd anticipated. For all she knew, George could have cursed at her and sent her packing. For him to welcome the idea of having fathered a child was beyond wonderful.

"Tell me why we broke up?" he asked.

"I don't know. I think we just got busy and went our separate ways. Nothing formally ended," she said.

"Yeah, I don't remember us actually having a breakup." He took a swallow of beer. "What would you think of us going out again?"

Ivy's heart jumped like a frog. "I, uh, gee … I sure didn't expect all this."

"So, that's a yes? You'll go out with me? And I can meet Luna?"

"Of course. I'd be delighted. And you sure can meet Luna. You're her daddy!" Ivy giggled.

George reached for her and carried her into a hug, then he kissed her briefly on the lips. "By the way, we only did it once. And we produced a baby?"

"Someone told me once is enough."

"Well, I guess that's true. Look what happened!"

Ivy and George shared a laugh.

THIRTY-THREE

LATISHA WAS STIRRING a sizable amount of sugar into her iced tea as she spoke. "I can't believe everything that's happened this year. Not the least being your accident."

"Yes, that was incredible, the impact, being pushed out of the way of that truck like we were flies in the air." Bobbi shook her head at the memory. "We all were fortunate to survive that wreck. Except for my car. My poor baby died that day."

"But you have a really nice new car," Hillary said.

"Oh, it's wonderful, but I liked the one that got totaled better."

"You were so lucky not to have been seriously injured," Abby told her. "The way that giant truck slammed into your side of the car, you could have been crushed."

"I know. I am so grateful. And grateful no one else was hurt, too."

"How is Ivy doing with the new baby?" Latisha asked.

"Very well, much to my surprise," Bobbi replied. "She has become this organized, super mom. I am so impressed with her. Mrs. York has been a godsend, too. Everything is right with Ivy."

"Tell them the other news," Abby prompted.

HAIRCUT AND HIGHLIGHTS

"Well, of all things, Ivy is seeing the baby's father. Can you imagine that happened?" Bobbi asked. "He didn't know anything about the baby until she told him."

"Nope," Latisha said, "I would have bet money he would run."

"They've been dating seriously for several weeks. But the best news is, George loves the baby. Well, it is *his* baby. He's been spending time with Luna, doting on her; it's all so cute." Bobbi smiled happily.

"Is he going to support the baby?" Hillary asked.

"He's been giving money to Ivy, but I think his plans are more permanent than that," Bobbi hinted.

"You mean *marriage?*" Latisha asked.

"Yes. I think he wants to marry Ivy, eventually. In the meantime, he's providing for his baby," Bobbie replied. "I couldn't ask for more."

"I'm just so over the moon happy for her," Abby said.

"How does Ivy feel about all of this?" Hillary asked.

"She's walking on a cloud every morning when she comes to work. Her smile extends from one side of the salon to the other. That girl is one happy mama," Abby told her.

"George is a nice young man," Bobbie added. "And he makes good money in his craft. He can support a family."

"Well, I'm happy for the girl," Latisha smiled. "Those situations don't usually work out any too well."

"You are very right, Latisha," Bobbie agreed. "Ivy is fortunate. Blessed, perhaps."

"Any word about Rose?" Hillary asked Abby.

"No, I'm afraid not." Abby shrugged. "I guess I'll never know what happened to her."

"I keep saying, she skipped town. Those types don't stay put," Latisha said.

"Those 'types' are individuals, human beings. We don't know what could have happened. Yes, maybe she left town. She could have had a reason for that. But other things could have occurred." Abby was irritated with the other woman's constant negative attitude about the homeless but tried to not let it show.

"Such as? What do *you* think happened to her?" Bobbi asked.

"I don't know. I can only speculate. Maybe she was in an accident and has been in rehab. Maybe she got off the street." Abby flipped her hands in the air in exasperation.

"Maybe she just up and left town," suggested Latisha.

Abby turned toward the woman who had so many opinions. "Latisha, I'm tired of your negative views on the homeless. Rose is different. She's a good person, I know that in my heart."

"Humph," Latisha grunted before she took a sip of tea.

"Let's change the subject," Hillary suggested. "How's your love life, Abby?"

"Nonexistent. Nada." Abby thought whether to share more and decided why not? "I've been getting visits from my ex. Unexpected, uninvited visits."

"You're kidding!" Bobbi exclaimed.

"I'm afraid not. Three times. The last time he was drunk, and my fireman neighbor had to escort him out of the building."

Hillary shot an impressed look at her. "Really?"

"Don't get any ideas. We're just neighbors … maybe acquaintances." She couldn't help that her lips curled up at the corners.

"Isn't he a hunk?" Bobbie asked.

"Yes, he's definitely a hunk. Well built, handsome, and very nice from what I've seen," Abby replied.

"I would go after that," Hillary suggested. "Don't pass up what's right under your nose."

"The timing hasn't been right," Abby said. "I don't know."

"Make the timing right. Go get him," Hillary said.

"We'll see."

"How's *your* love life, Hillary?" Latisha asked.

"I had been enjoying spending time with my boyfriend…"

"But?" Abby asked.

"I'm getting bored with him." Hillary shrugged.

"How is that? I thought you loved him?" Bobbie asked.

"I did. But now that he's finally come around to my thinking, I've discovered he's boring."

"Boring? Girl, you crazy," Latisha said. "This guy breaks your heart; you take him back. He runs around with another woman; you take him back. He does it again; you take him back. Now that he's committed to you, you think he's boring. Ump, you one crazy woman." Latisha shook her head.

Hillary sat silently, not commenting on the string of scenarios that were all true.

"Don't worry about it, Hillary," Abby said, touching her arm. "You'll know what to do when the time is right. Who knows? You may have a change of heart."

"I don't think so. I was planning to break it off sometime this week," Hillary said. "Oh well, onward and upward." She graced them with a smile.

Latisha shook her head.

THIRTY-FOUR

ROSE STOOD before the big gas stove, sufficiently sized to accommodate the many mouths it had to feed. She stirred the vegetable soup with a wooden spoon. It had been her idea to create vegetable soup. She included pieces of leftover chicken to make it hearty, and macaroni. The soup smelled delicious with all the spices she'd added.

"Rose, we're hungry! Snap it up!" called one of the women seated at the long dining room table. All those waiting had returned from work and, no doubt, had worked up appetites.

"Yeah, I'm dishing it up now," Rose called from the kitchen. "You could come take some bowls in there."

Marie, a large woman who'd been an addict when on the street, until she entered the program, came into the kitchen. "Give me some bowls."

"Put them on that tray on the counter," Rose instructed.

Marie placed four bowls on the tray and transported them to the dining room. Rose took four more on another tray and brought them to the diners. Patti asked who was saying grace.

"I will," Rose said. "Holy Father, thank you for all we have learned today. We are grateful for Your protection and appreciate Your guidance as we take our steps back to a normal life. Please bless this food to the nourishment of our bodies. In Jesus' name. Amen."

"You always do nice grace," Patti stated.

"Thanks," Rose said. "I just say what's in my heart."

"Someone said you were leaving," remarked Marie, stirring her soup around with a spoon.

"I hope to. I have to contact someone first," Rose said, her spoon halfway to her mouth.

"That lady you said would help you?" asked Patti.

"Yes, her. I haven't done it yet because I wanted to wait until I felt I was established in my job. I can't just land on her doorstep and expect she'll take me in."

"Not a good idea," Lois advised. She was also a recovering drug addict, making real strides to turn her life around.

Grace entered the dining room as if she were looking for something or someone. "Greetings, ladies. How is dinner?"

"Yummy," Libby said between slurps of soup. "I like the bread, too." Libby was a little flabby, so she really needed to eat more soup and less bread. Her life on the street had been brutal. She had been pimped out by her boyfriend. Many a night she'd returned to him bruised and battered.

The other women echoed Libby's sentiments.

"Good. Glad to hear it." Grace pulled out a chair to sit at the table. "Anyone need anything? Any questions?"

The women either grunted an answer as they ate or said no.

"Okay then. I have reports to write, so I'll be in my office." Grace stood. "Has anyone seen my clipboard?"

"I saw it on the table in the hallway. It's on the shelf below," Rose said.

"No wonder I didn't see it. Thank you, Rose." Grace left the dining room to retrieve her clipboard.

"Who's doing cleanup?" Marie asked as she set her spoon on the placemat.

"I was last night," Libby responded.

"I think it's me and Andrea, except she's not here," Flo said. "I guess she had to work late." Flo had the biggest, roundest eyes. The sorrow she bore from being on the street was easy to read. She had been a meth addict, and it showed on her face and body.

"I'll help you," Rose volunteered.

"But you cooked," Flo said.

"So what? I can help cleanup, too." Rose smiled at her.

The two women gathered the bowls and utensils onto the trays and transported everything into the kitchen.

"I'll wash," said Flo. "You dry."

"You look like you're gaining weight," Rose said, taking a dish towel to the bowls and stacking them until she placed them on the shelf.

"Yes, I've gained ten pounds. But my face is still so thin. My eyes bug out and my cheeks are practically pointed." Flo kept scrubbing the bowls as she talked. "And my skin!"

"Oh, it's not that bad. I can see the difference, even in your face," Rose told her with a smile. "Just give it some time. You'll fatten up and no one will ever guess you were on meth." That wasn't an entirely true statement. Some of the sores on her face had faded, but others didn't appear to be diminishing. Rose thought the woman might end up with scarring from her drug habit.

"I've been feeling like bugs are crawling under my skin. I can feel them right now," Flo said, pulling her hands out of the water and scratching her left arm. "The counselor said it was part of my addiction; a delusion, I think she called it. But it sure feels real to me. I could just scratch my skin off. Do you see anything?" She stuck her arm toward Rose.

"Nothing, Flo. I don't see anything." Rose thanked God that she never tried meth. No high was worth this effect. She remembered some of the people on the street, incredibly skinny, appearing confused, like they had no idea what was happening. Some of them couldn't string words into a sentence. And the sores on their faces and lips were disgusting to look at.

"How are you able to work?" she asked.

"My job is very simple. How hard can doing laundry be?" she said with a laugh. "I don't meet a lot of people in the basement of the hospital. I have supervisors who look out for me, so I manage to work pretty well. It's better than being on the street, and I am being a responsible person. That was important to me, to be responsible again. Some of my agitation may fade eventually, they say. Then I can do something else, maybe." She shrugged as she placed the bread plate on the draining board.

"I hope things go well for you," Rose said with a small smile.

"Thanks."

Rose finished putting away the dishes, then went to her room. She rummaged around in her suitcase, looking for a card, which she found among other small items she kept in a plastic zipper bag. Rose held the card between two fingers, reading the name on it: Abby Bugsly. Should she call her now? It was early evening. What would she have to say? Would Abby be welcoming? Maybe she would reject Rose's proposal? It was asking a lot. But she had offered to help her. She had said not to hesitate to call her. So, why was she hesitating? The worst that could happen was she said no. But a no would send Rose into depression. It would devastate her.

There wasn't a Plan B. Just Plan A, to room with Abby. She could pay half the rent, save up for a car. It was workable. She wasn't being delusional like Flo, was she? This really could happen, right? Rose wasn't being naïve. She had never been naïve her entire life. No, this was her plan, and she was going to see it through. Rose would call Abby. Tonight.

… Maybe.

THIRTY-FIVE

IVY BOUNCED INTO THE SALON. Everyone turned their head toward the door to see what had breezed in with such gusto.

"My, aren't you effervescent today," Abby commented as she washed a woman's hair.

Ivy beamed, flinging out her arms. "I have an announcement!"

"What?" Sonia asked as she stood teasing her client's hair.

"I'm getting married!" Ivy said. "I'm so happy, I could bust!"

She received a round of applause from the women in their varying phases of transformation.

"Congratulations, Ivy," Abby said. "When did this happen?"

"George proposed last night. Look!" Ivy thrust out her hand to show the diamond on her ring finger.

"Wow, a sparkler," Sonia said with appreciation. "I jealous."

Abby wrapped her client's hair in a towel and left her at the shampoo bowl so she could see the ring. "Oh, it's absolutely gorgeous, Ivy!"

"When you marry?" Sonia asked, smoothing the top layer of hair over the teased sections.

"Soon, very soon. We don't want to wait. Maybe a justice of

HAIRCUT AND HIGHLIGHTS

the peace, or at the courthouse." Ivy slung her backpack under her station. "Nothing fancy. We don't need fancy, just the ceremony." She gave everyone a smile.

"I'm so happy for you." Abby took Ivy into a warm embrace. "You and your baby deserve this."

"I want you to stand up with me when we get married," Ivy said.

"I'd be so pleased to do that," Abby said, fighting back tears of joy.

"What about your dress?" Sonia asked.

"Aunt Bobbie said she has a vintage one that is darling that she'll give me. I think she said it was from the sixties. It's street length and has lace. Hey, what else could I ask for?" Ivy asked with a big smile.

Abby had never seen her smile so much within a short period of time. "I'm sure it will be lovely."

The bell over the door clanged and in walked Ruby. She gawked around the room as if looking for someone. "I thought Penelope would be here."

"I haven't seen her today. Sometimes, she comes late or forgets she has an appointment," Abby said. She didn't see how they had become friends, although they both lived at the Breezeway Condominium.

"Well, we were going to lunch after she's done here. I wonder what happened."

"I have no idea, Ruby."

"Hmm, guess I'll go home. Tell her if you see her, I went home, okay?" Ruby asked.

"I will."

During her lunch break, Ivy stopped by a sweet little white church on Peninsula Drive. It had attracted her attention when she and Mrs. York were out shopping. The area was replete with gorgeous old homes. Ivy would give her little left toe to own one of them. She loved the old- time appearance of the mansions and how they backed up to the Halifax River. And right in the middle of all this grandeur proudly stood the church. Even though aged, it blended with the old mansions. It had the classic steeple, and a bell hanging in the belfry. The church looked romantic in Ivy's eyes, like something from yesterday, with a history to tell. Vintage. Like her dress.

When she walked through the heavy wooden front door, she was immediately able to see wooden pews organized in groups to the left and right of the aisle. They were family pews where numerous members could sit together, complete with a swinging half door as one entered the enclosure. Other pews were arranged in rows. The platform was all white, with an ornate podium in the center. Folding chairs were to the right where she imagined the choir sang. Two ornate chairs bookended the altar with its golden trays, candleholders, and cross in the center.

She sat in the back pew, gazing at the golden framed picture of Jesus.

"May I help you?" a masculine voice asked.

"Oh, you startled me." Ivy's hand jumped to her throat.

"I'm so sorry. What can I do for you?" He wore a clerical collar under a white open-necked shirt. His hair almost matched the shirt.

"I'm engaged, and I was hoping someone in this church could marry us. I'm not a member, but I love this church. It's so sweet, romantic, and old. I like old things. This church looks like it has history," she said, rambling on in her nervousness. "Are you the pastor?"

"Yes, I am. My name is Pastor Mathews. And I am old, too." He chuckled when he made the last remark.

"Pastor Mathews, would you marry us?" she asked, a pleading look taking over her expression. "Please?"

"When do you want to do the nuptials?"

"This weekend? Is that too soon?" Ivy couldn't help thinking, "Who asks to be married within a few days?"

"No, dear. I can marry you on Saturday. What time would you like?"

"That's wonderful! You don't know what this means to me! Time? Uh, eleven? My fiancé will be thrilled, too." Thinking she should ask permission before she acted, she said, "May I hug you?"

The pastor laughed. "Of course, you may."

Ivy jumped up and threw her arms around the minister. "Thank you, thank you so much!"

Gently, he pushed her away after a bit. "Follow me into the office and we'll fill out all the paperwork."

Ivy followed the pastor into his office, the first steps into her new life.

———

The phone rang, startling Abby as she lay on the couch with Seely, watching TV.

"Hello?"

"Hey, it's Ruby," the voice said on the other end. "I thought you should know, so I'm calling."

"Know what?"

"Penelope died. She had a big heart attack in the garden while walking with her husband," Ruby replied.

"No! How awful."

"Yeah, well, she was up in years. Like me. You never know when it's going to happen," she said, sounding morose.

"I'm so sorry for your loss, Ruby."

"We hadn't been friends for a lot of years or anything, but we were finally friends. Before that, we always argued. She didn't understand me, and I have to admit, I didn't understand her."

"Well, I'm sorry to hear this. I'll check the book to see if she's scheduled anywhere," Abby said.

"Okay, Abby, I'm just passing the word. Have a good night."

Ruby hung up.

Abby looked at the cat grooming herself. She had darkened a great deal since her arrival. Once a snowball, she was now very dark around her face, ears, and tail. Her body had darkened slightly, but still appeared creamy, with dark stockings.

"I lost a customer, Seely. Sad. She was a quiet lady. I'm sure her husband will miss her."

The cat meowed as if she understood the words spoken.

Then the phone rang again. It was Jack, of all people!

"Hi," she said hesitantly.

"Hey. I thought you should know who that spit sample you gave me belongs to."

"Yes, please tell me."

"It was a clear match to the second blood type we found at that murder scene," he said in a professional voice.

"The killer's blood matches the spit?" she asked in disbelief.

"Definitely."

"Oh. That's not good. I mean, I've seen him hanging around my salon more than once," she said, feeling queasy.

"If you see him again, call 911 immediately."

"I will, of course. Who is he?"

"A guy named Sheppard Green. Street name is Shep. A nasty character with ties to drugs and organized crime some years back." She heard Jack rustling papers. "Don't get near him."

"I'm not stupid, Jack."

"I mean it. Don't go sleuthing."

"Trust me, I won't. Are you going to arrest him?" She was hoping for a quick arrest.

"If we can find him," he replied. "We've got bodies out there looking for him. All my informants are on the alert, too."

"That's good to know."

"All right, I just thought you should know for your protection," he said. "Good night."

Abby clicked off her phone, glancing at the door to see if the deadbolt was turned. It was. "Let's go to bed, Seely. I've had enough excitement."

THIRTY-SIX

SHE WAS HESITATING EVEN though she had been told not to. Rose summoned up her courage. It felt like it was lying down in her feet, the effort was so great, and that was only because the alternative answer she desperately dreaded would devastate her. But she punched in the numbers printed on the card and prayed.

"Hello," Abby said into her phone.

"Hi, Abby, it's Rose. Remember me?" She half expected Abby had forgotten her.

"*Rose*! Where have you been? I've been so worried about you," came the words in a rush. "Are you okay?"

"I'm fine. More than fine. I'm off the street."

"Really? That's wonderful!"

"I'm in transitional housing after being at the shelter," she explained. "I haven't been on the street for probably six months or so. I even have a job."

"A *job*? Wow, blow me over. I am totally thrilled for you."

"Yeah, I work at a big telephone company doing clerical work. It's a good job with benefits. I like the job a lot," she said. "They seem to like me, so I'm on my way to being independent."

HAIRCUT AND HIGHLIGHTS

"Everything sounds wonderful, Rose. I'm so happy for you and proud of you. When can I see you?"

"How about today? Coffee at the deli on the corner?"

"Around two would be good for me," Abby said.

"I'll meet you then. I can take my lunch at that time."

"I'll look forward to seeing you, Rose."

Two o'clock couldn't come soon enough for Abby. She was so eager to see Rose after all the time that had gone by. She couldn't help but wonder how she looked, was she healthy, and had she really straightened her life around? She had promised to help Rose, and then the woman disappeared. What had happened to cause that?

Just before two o'clock, Abby left the salon and walked to the deli. She stepped inside, glancing around the mostly empty tables. There sat another version of Rose at one of them.

Abby rushed over to the table. "Look at you! You're gorgeous!" Abby flung both arms out to hug Rose after she stood to greet her. "My goodness, you look fabulous!"

Rose was wearing a soft green, two-piece cotton dress with green sling backs, and she looked radiant. Not only did her skin glow, she was wearing makeup. Her enhanced features made her look prettier, and her hair was just like Abby had styled it. Rose looked similar to every other professional woman working downtown.

"No one would ever guess you lived on the street at one time," Abby said.

"Thank you. I've worked hard to return to the old Rose, the one I used to be before hard times hit. Except I'm better than the old Rose. The new improved version is wiser and has coping skills to fall back on." Rose sat back in her chair.

Abby sat across from her. "The shelter did amazing things for you."

"I know. Total strangers took me in, cared about me, cared for me, and pointed me in a healthy direction. I couldn't be more grateful," she said. When she saw a server, she raised her hand.

The server came over immediately.

"Two coffees, please." Turning back to Abby, Rose said, "I came in here one time, and that waitress right there refused to wait on me. I guess I look different today."

"I'm sure you do. So, tell me, why did you disappear?" Abby asked. She couldn't wait any longer to hear the details.

Rose explained about witnessing Sam being murdered in front of Abby's salon and how, in fear, she went to the shelter for help. She told her about the counseling sessions and life skills she'd learned, and how she finally came to realize her father was the cause of her emotional pain and low self-esteem. While her father's unfortunate behavior was obviously the root cause, Rose had not recognized the emotional damage she carried was not of her doing. She'd believed as an adult that she was worthless.

"Now, I share a room with Patti Miracle, who's a former street person, too. She's had it hard, has scars on her face and arms. But she's trying to better herself, move on to her own place." Rose accepted her coffee from the server, then poured cream into the cup.

Abby added sweetener and cream to her coffee. "So, what are your plans, Rose? Do you want to get your own place, too?" She took a sip.

"Yes, I would like my own place, but I'd really like to share an apartment with someone first. That way, I could save money for a car, so I don't have to take the bus," Rose answered, raising the cup to her lips.

"That's a good idea. Is there anyone you can room with?"

"Maybe you? You said you'd help me." Rose looked at her with a hopeful expression.

Abby didn't say anything at first. It was true, she had promised to help this woman. Taking her in as a roommate would be helping a lot. She stalled her answer by drinking more coffee. Did she want to open her living quarters to a former homeless person? Did she want to have a roommate? It wasn't like she had expensive jewelry. Eric had sold anything of value long ago to feed his alcohol habit. She really didn't have a lot of valuables. So, what was her hesitation?

"I know this is sudden. I'm putting you on the spot. I'm sorry. This might be asking too much of you," Rose said.

"No, Rose. I'm just surprised. Like you said, it's sudden. I didn't know what happened to you until just now. And I did offer to help you, and I want to. Really, I do. Can we give this a minute to sink in?"

"Oh, of course. Let it sink in. This whole situation is crazy. My father, my becoming homeless, living on the street … now I'm in transitional housing, for crying out loud. I'm a crazy mess. Why would anyone want to be involved with me, let alone live with me? I'm sorry, Abby. I overstepped. Forget I said anything. You've been kind to me, but what I asked is over the top … too much. I get it." Rose stood to leave.

"No, don't leave. Sit back down." Abby reached out a hand to stop Rose.

The woman returned to her seat.

"You can move in with me, Rose. As soon as you want. Today. I don't care." Abby folded her arms over the table, looking directly into Rose's face. "Let's see how it goes. If either one of us is uncomfortable, finds the other one's habits annoying, then we call it off. How does that sound?"

"That sounds fine. Who knows, *you* might be really annoying to live with," Rose joked.

Abby laughed. "You never know, do you? I could snore loud

enough for you to hear me across the hall." They shared a laugh.

"Oh, I do have a cat. You have to accept cats, that's nonnegotiable."

"Not a problem. I love cats. I've had several."

"And your bedroom is small."

"I share a small room now. One all to myself is a step up."

Abby held her hand out across the table. "Deal?"

"Deal," Rose said, shaking her hand.

"Oh, one thing I need to tell you. About the murder. The police know who killed Sam. DNA from blood and spit. Some guy named Sheppard Green. Did you know that was the guy who killed Sam?"

"Yes. I knew him, too. Except we called him Shep." Rose swallowed heavily before going on. "I stood there, hiding behind a dumpster, watching Shep kill Sam."

Abby was stunned by that news. "That must have been awful. I didn't know till recently the victim was your boyfriend. Okay. Well, they're looking for him to arrest. I've seen him around my salon. Several times. He even came inside and spit on the door when leaving."

"I'm sure he's looking for me," Rose said, eyes widening.

"You need to be very careful until they arrest him," Abby warned.

"I will. But I'm still moving in. I'm not letting that guy control my life." Rose looked determined as she spoke the words. "No one is controlling me but me."

"Whatever you're comfortable doing."

"This isn't about comfort. It's about being strong."

Judging by Rose's attitude and words, she had changed a great deal since Abby saw her last. "You need to tell the police about witnessing the murder."

Rose did not respond.

THIRTY-SEVEN

IT WAS SATURDAY MORNING, Ivy's wedding day. Abby roused herself out of bed and headed to the kitchen to make coffee. While it was brewing, she stepped into the second bedroom. With the exception of a suitcase and carry-on bag, the room was empty. Abby picked up the two articles and carried them into her bedroom. Rose was moving in this afternoon. She had high hopes this arrangement would work out—for both their sakes.

Abby shoved the suitcase into the bottom of her closet and slid the carry-on up to the shelf. Pulling out a pink dress, she hung it on the closet door, then went to retrieve a cup of coffee. Seely, a little late in her morning routine, came whining into the kitchen.

"I know, you're hungry. Chow's coming right up."

Abby placed fresh water and kitty nuggets on the floor, which Seely quickly pounced on.

While in the bathroom, she applied makeup and brushed her long hair. The last thing she had to do was get into her dress. Since the reception was on the beach, she chose slip-on sandals to wear. Abby looked at herself in the full-length mirror affixed to the backside of the bedroom door, and approved the image reflected. Pink was always a good color for her fair complexion. The color also complimented her blonde hair.

"Okay, Miss Seely, I will see you later," she said to the cat as she walked to the front door.

Once in her car, she crossed the Main Street Bridge to the beach side of Daytona. It was a very high bridge, allowing the driver to enjoy a breathtaking view of the river and the ocean in the distance while descending to the other side. It didn't take long to reach the church because the street was located just as she exited the bridge. Once parked, she entered the beautiful old building.

"Where is Ivy?" she asked inside the vestibule to no one in particular.

A woman turned around quickly. "Abby, you're here! Ivy is in that room over there, waiting for you." She pointed. "I'm trying to get people organized." The young woman talking had blue hair, so Abby figured she was also a hairdresser.

"Okay, I'll go over there." Abby walked toward the room, pulling the drape to the side so she could enter. It felt stuffy. "Aren't you hot in here?" she asked, seeing Ivy standing in the center of the room.

"Yes! Roasting!" she answered, her face flushed bright red. "Tell Britney to get this show rolling."

"Blue-hair Britney?" Abby asked.

"That's the one."

"On it."

Abby walked out and over to Britney. "Ivy says to get rolling."

Britney went into action. "Okay, people, get to your seats. It's time for the bride."

Everyone followed instructions quickly.

"Tell her we're ready," Britney instructed.

HAIRCUT AND HIGHLIGHTS

Abby walked back to the room, pulled open the drape, and said, "Come on out, bride. We're ready for you."

"Get in here," Ivy hissed, reaching for her arm. "You go out first, then I follow. Listen for the music, then go."

"Where am I going?"

"Down the aisle, slow, in time with the music, right? The pastor is up front. George will be in front of him. Go, go!" she said frantically.

I guess all brides get crazy on their wedding day.

Abby left the room and walked to the back of the church and waited. Someone she didn't know was seated at the organ and began to play. Abby started a slow trek down the aisle, pausing after each step until she reached the front, then stood near the pastor. She looked at George, who was handsome in a rented black tuxedo which, Abby thought, was a little fancy for the time of day, but what did she know?

The organist made her instrument sound like a flurry of horns and, magically, Ivy appeared at the top of the aisle. Everyone rose to their feet and watched as she slowly came down the aisle toward her husband-to-be. Her white dress covered her knees as it flared out from her waist. The bodice was covered in lace, surrounding the scoop neck, and the lace sleeves carried down to her wrists. A short veil extended from a floral headband that sat atop her auburn hair. She carried a small bouquet of pink roses. Ivy was beautiful to behold.

She joined George in front of the minister, taking his offered hand in hers. The ceremony began and was short and sweet. Abby held back tears of joy.

Afterwards, everyone hugged the bride and groom, and delivered wishes of joy and a long successful marriage, then they headed to the beach for the reception. Abby had closed the salon so Sonia could attend and any clients who were invited, although it was her understanding that this would be a small affair. Much to her surprise, she saw more people joining the gathering on the beach than had been at the wedding. A lot more! She started greeting those she knew from the salon.

A cabana had been erected to cover the food, especially the cake. A few umbrellas were also placed around to shade those not wanting to be in the sun. It was a very bright day at the beach and Abby quickly felt the intensity of the rays touching her skin, and it wasn't even noon.

The waves rolled in lazily, adding a backup choir to the loud hip-hop music being pumped from some device. Abby wondered if they had gotten approval from the hotel to hold a party on their portion of the beach.

She indulged in a glass of champagne and munched some cheese cubes and olives. She watched with amusement as some of the young couples danced in the waves, despite wearing skirts and jeans. They didn't seem to mind getting wet as they frolicked amid the frothy water. One young girl was so intent on flirting with a guy in shorts and a tee-shirt clinging to his chest that she got drenched by a larger than usual wave which had caught her above the waist. She shrieked her way out of the deluge onto dryer territory.

Yes, I was that silly, too, back then. From a distance, Abby watched as the happy couple cut the cake and politely exchanged a taste with each other. After that, she decided she had best get home to help Rose move in.

Rose struggled up the stairs with her suitcase and sleeping bag. Everything she owned and valued was contained within the beat-up piece of luggage. Compared to a normal woman, she didn't own much if everything could be squeezed into one suitcase. She knocked on the door and waited.

"Rose! You're here!" Abby stood back from the door to let the woman enter. "Do you need help?"

"No, I got it. This is nothing compared to the staircase."

"Then follow me."

Abby escorted Rose to her new room. She flung her sleeping bag on the floor, then placed the suitcase near the closet.

"I never thought about you not having any furniture," Abby said, noting the sleeping bag. "Will that be comfortable enough?"

"It will do until I go to Goodwill. I can buy a bed and dresser cheap."

"Gee, I feel bad about you sleeping on the floor."

"No big deal. I used to sleep on your doorway."

"This is true."

Seely came out from her hiding place and announced herself loudly.

"Oh, she's so pretty. Aw, here kitty, what's your name?" Rose cooed, bending to pet the cat.

"Seely."

"Seely, my girl. Pretty girl," Rose said, petting the purring feline.

"She's going to love you if you keep petting her," Abby said with a grin.

"No problem. I love cats."

"Come on, I'll show you around," Abby said, leading the way.

"My bedroom." Abby gestured with her arm in that direction. "Obviously, the bathroom. There's room in the drawers for some of your things. I moved some of my stuff around." Walking a bit farther, she said, "And this is obviously the kitchen. There are plenty of cupboards, so you can easily store your food items. We can split the fridge. It's pretty roomy." She turned. "And, of course, this is the living room. There's a table against the wall if we need to host a dinner. I usually just sit on one of the stools under the counter when I eat."

"Yes, that's probably what I'll do, too."

"I go to the grocery once a week, so you can ride with me

until you get a car. And I'll take you bed shopping at Goodwill whenever you want to go."

"Sometime this week would be great."

"Okay, we'll do that."

"I do need a grocery run. I don't have any food."

"Come on, Rose, let's go shopping!"

THIRTY-EIGHT

BY THE NEXT WEEKEND, Rose had a bed, a nightstand, and dresser. Goodwill delivered everything, so Rose didn't have to stress about that. Her new bedroom—*her* very own bedroom--was quickly taking shape. Rose had stashed away as much money as possible to be able to afford furniture, sheets, and food for when she was able to be on her own. The sleeping bag had been gifted to her by the shelter.

Rose felt everything was falling into place. She wasn't far from her employment, so she only had to take one bus to work. She and Abby were getting along just fine, especially considering they really didn't know each other very well. Their eating times and bedtime routines seemed to coincide well, too. Rose thought Abby was going out of her way to make her comfortable and feel welcome. Her efforts were working.

This was paradise for Rose.

———

Abby sat on her bed, thinking about the new arrangement. As an adult, she had always lived by herself, except when she was married. Not ever having roommates before, Rose was an adjustment to make. But she was bending over backwards to accommodate the woman, to give her a chance to succeed. She didn't want to look back on this unique situation and think, "I could have done more. I could have made this transition easier for her."

The rest was up to Rose. She was the one who had to rise to the challenge of starting a new life. Abby couldn't do that for her. No one had stepped in to make things easier for her either when she'd returned to Daytona Beach to start over. She had to meet that challenge by herself. *Some things we just have to accomplish singularly.*

So far, Rose's habits weren't irritating or so completely opposite that it caused a problem. They were getting along well. Their sense of humors blended, and neither was so sensitive the other had to carefully walk around for fear of offending. *This could work out well.* Abby smiled to herself as she pondered this new arrangement.

Two weeks later, Rose left for work. She had to hurry because she was running later than normal. After twisting her ankle when her heel caught in a crack in the sidewalk, Rose limped to the bus stop across from where she lived in time to board the bus. She took the closest seat, reaching down to massage her ankle when settled. *Stupid heels.*

As she sat back against the bench seat, her eyes caught sight of a homeless man. And he wasn't just any homeless man lurking by the building she lived in. It was Shep. She hadn't seen him since he came to the shelter with two other men. Shep hanging around the building she lived in was not a good sign. *Abby was right. He must know I live here*! That thought and seeing him made her tremble.

HAIRCUT AND HIGHLIGHTS

Rose thought about her job. That job was everything to her. She didn't need Shep ruining her life. No, she wouldn't allow that to happen. Rose pulled on her coping techniques, pushing away the negative, what she had no control over. Instead, she thought about how she'd felt when she first started her employment, how she'd wondered if she could handle the job. Would she feel pressured to perform? *Could* she perform after years away from the workplace? Had being homeless wrecked her chances for success?

But the answers came quickly in the form of the welcoming people she worked with. Each was helpful when she was at a loss due to a new situation arising. Her supervisor was kind to her, evidently understanding that Rose might require more patience from her than other new employees. When she felt stressed back then, Rose had thought about the tools she had been given during counseling sessions. This situation was no different. She soldiered on then, and would do so now. Her path was laid out; all she had to do was walk.

Of course, it was normal for Rose to feel apprehensive at times. Everyone did, that was part of life. But her biggest fear was her past rearing its ugly head. What would she do if she suddenly felt her self-esteem flowing like water from a faucet into the drain? When Rose had shared her fears with Abby, she had said, "Do it afraid. Trust in the Lord to help."

Rose looked out the window across the aisle. *Do it afraid.* She could do that. She had done that. Fear wasn't an unfamiliar emotion. She had conquered getting off the street. Surely, she could handle any blip on her path. Even Shep. All her fears compared to being on the street paled in comparison. *I've got this covered.*

Abby chose to sleep in one morning because her book had appointments beginning at one. She stretched, disturbing Seely who was sleeping snugly beside her.

"Meow," the cat fussed.

"Oh, you've had enough sleep," Abby said to the cat, stroking her body. "You live a privileged life, my dear kitty."

Abby flung off the covers and got out of bed, further disturbing Seely. After her bathroom duties were completed, Abby made coffee. After it had brewed, she languished on the couch, cup in hand. She heard someone walk heavily up the stairs, sounding like they were wearing boots. "Must be Mark," she said to Seely. "My neighbor is coming home." Abby imagined him in uniform, looking handsome and rugged.

A knock at the door startled her. She got up, pulling her bathrobe closer. "I'm coming, Mark."

Abby opened the door wide. Standing before her was not Mark, but the homeless man she had seen inside and outside her salon. The one who'd committed murder in front of her salon. *Shep!* He was dressed in ratty fatigues with a Vietnam insignia on the crummy cap covering his head. His hacked beard and unkempt long hair made Abby think of bugs crawling inside. The man's breath was so atrocious, she could smell it three feet away, mingled with the stench of his body.

Abby's stomach jumped. "May I help you?" she asked, not wanting to upset him in case he was mentally unbalanced.

When he spoke, she got a whiff of the liquor on his breath, overriding his noxious body odor for a moment. "Rose here?" he asked.

Suddenly feeling the need to protect her roommate, she lied, even though she wasn't a good liar. "I don't know anyone by that name."

"Yes, you do," he insisted, spittle spraying from his mouth. "She lives here. I seen her."

Her heart clenched in her throat. "You must be mistaken. She doesn't live here."

The man's eyes narrowed as they penetrated into her. He seemed larger than life, as if he had morphed into a hovering prehistoric creature. And here she stood, in her bathrobe, defenseless.

"Where is Rose?" he growled.

"Not here, I told you. Now leave, or I'll call the police." This was a bluff. Her phone was in the bedroom, totally out of reach to hit 911.

The smelly man stepped toward her, his massive shoulders sending the door bouncing against the wall as he came inside. Abby backed up to get out of his path. He continued toward her, his heavy boots hitting on the wooden floors as he slammed the door behind him with such force, it bounced open.

Abby attempted a smile, putting both hands in front of her. "Please, you don't want to do this. You'll get into trouble, go to jail. None of that will be pleasant."

The hulking man snorted, taking two more steps towards Abby.

"Look, this is all a big misunderstanding," she said, spreading out her arms. "You can turn around and leave right now, and I'll forget all about this. Never happened." She flipped one hand into the air and gave him a big smile. "Really. No memory."

One side of the man's lips tugged sideways. "Liar."

Abby didn't know how to proceed. She had tried talking, but that wasn't working. The only thing left was to physically defend herself. But how was she to do that against such a behemoth? She didn't have a weapon, not even a heavy piece of glass or metal decorating her tables to use as a substitute. In desperation, she continued backing toward the hallway where she might be able to run into her bedroom and lock the door. Maybe. If she could distract him, stop his trek for a few seconds, his dangerous approach. The malicious glare in his black eyes told her all she needed to know: he was going to kill her. Just like Rose's boyfriend.

Knowing she couldn't physically stop this man, she glanced to the side at the three bar stools tucked under the counter. *There is my weapon.* Taking a big step backwards, she reached to the side, grabbing two legs in her hands, and throwing the stool at her assailant.

Turning quickly to the left, she ran four steps into her bedroom and slammed the door. The lock turned with a click. Flinging herself onto the bed where her phone was, she snatched it, and pressed 911. When the operator answered, she could no doubt hear this behemoth in the background shouting and banging his fists on the door. Curses followed as he bellowed and banged his dissatisfaction over being blocked from his intended purpose.

"He's breaking the door down; I see it giving way," she cried frantically into the phone. "I have no defense if he gets through the door!"

Abby was told to stay on the phone, that officers were en route.

She looked frantically around her bedroom for a weapon. The best she could find was a pair of manicure scissors. Looking at the puny scissors in her hand, she felt at a loss to defend herself. Suddenly, she knew what to do.

"Jesus, help me!" she cried out loudly.

After one more bang on the door, she heard another man's voice coming from the other side, and a skirmish began. She knew a fight was taking place in her hallway because, amid grunts, bodies were thudding from one side of the wall over to the other. She heard a picture fall to the floor, and footsteps racing over the wooden floors. Additional grunting and a few curses ensued, then more shouting and colliding with the walls. It sounded like a team of burly football players were wrestling on the other side.

"You're under arrest," declared another male voice, obviously belonging to a police officer.

Then everything quieted down for a few seconds.

A soft knock on the door resounded. "You can come out. It's safe."

Abby unlocked the door and opened it. There stood Mark with a bloody lip and his hair askew, one strap of his suspenders having slipped off his white tee-shirt. She couldn't believe he was standing in her hallway.

"Mark? How did you know?"

"I heard the doors slamming and then that big brute making a ruckus. I knew you were in trouble," he said with a small smile, despite the bleeding lip. "You're never this noisy."

Abby ran into his arms, placing her head on his muscular chest. "Oh, Mark. You are an answer to a prayer."

"Ma'am?" a small voice asked.

Abby realized the dispatcher was still on the line. "I'm so sorry. The police came and I'm fine. Thank you," she said and clicked off.

"I knew the police couldn't get here so fast, so I had to step in, or you'd probably be toast," Mark said solemnly.

"Definitely. You saved my life."

"Ma'am," an officer said from the living room, "I need to take your statement."

"Of course." Abby stepped away from Mark.

"And yours," he said, pointing at Mark with his pen.

Both of them sat on the couch while they relayed their stories of what had happened. The officer wrote feverish notes as they spoke.

"Sign at the bottom," he directed when finished, handing the papers to them. "You can go about your normal business now."

Mark and Abby looked at each other, questioning that.

THIRTY-NINE

WHEN ABBY finally went to work, Sonia and Ivy were full of questions.

"We saw the police arrive and run into the building," Ivy said.

"We knew it had to be you," Sonia said. "What happen?"

Abby relayed the whole story to all the eager listeners in the salon.

"So, Mark came to your rescue?" Ivy asked.

"Yes. If he hadn't been home and heard the racket, I'd be dead for sure," Abby said.

"*Ay caramba!*" Sonia dramatically waved her arms over her head.

"What happens now?" Ivy asked, hands on her hips.

"I'll have to testify in court," Abby replied, sitting in the chair at her station. "And after I tell Rose what happened, I have to convince her to testify, too. She witnessed him murder her boyfriend."

"She not want to testify?" Sonia asked.

"I don't think the homeless like to turn on each other. One of those 'rules' of the street."

"But she not homeless now," Sonia reasoned.

"I know. I hope that will make a difference," Abby responded.

Abby was making spaghetti when Rose came home. As she stirred the pot of sauce, she looked at her roommate. "Hey. How was your day?"

"Okay," she answered, walking down the hallway to her room. "What happened to the walls and your door?" she asked as she walked along. Dark smudges decorated the walls and door, and the door jamb was buckling. The picture that had fallen was still on the floor, a jagged break crossing the glass.

"Long story. Come back here when you're ready, and I'll tell you all about it."

Rose returned quickly and sat on one of the stools. "I'm all ears. But it looks like there was a fight in the hallway," she said with a grin. "Who'd you beat up?"

Abby swung her eyes away from the sauce over to Rose. "There was a fight all right, but I didn't cause the mess."

"For real?"

Abby told Rose about Shep arriving at the door and intimidating her to gain entry.

"He asked specifically for you, Rose."

Rose sat silently, looking wide-eyed.

"The only weapon I had was that stool you're sitting on. After I threw it at him, I was able to get into my bedroom and lock the door. But he was determined to get in."

She told Rose about the racket he made, calling the police, and hearing the fight in the hallway. Rose didn't say a word at any point. "When I opened the door, I saw my neighbor standing there. If he hadn't heard the noise, I'd be dead, Rose."

She still didn't say anything.

"The police arrested him and took him to jail." Abby paused, coming around the counter to stand in front of her roommate. "Rose, I know this is the man you saw kill your boyfriend. He's also the one I've seen hanging around my salon."

Rose hung her head. "I saw him this morning hanging around outside when I was on the bus. I'm so sorry."

"I will have to testify as to what happened today. He's charged with attempted murder Rose," Abby said with a sigh. "You also need to testify to what you saw when he committed murder."

"*Me?*"

"Of course, *you.*"

"I can't. Just can't." Rose shook her head furiously as she spoke the words.

"He killed a man, Rose. *He murdered your boyfriend.* Right in front of you. You saw it go down. He needs to be put away for life."

Rose let out a long sigh.

"I told the police he was the one they're looking for. And I mentioned that you witnessed the murder of your boyfriend," Abby said.

Rose looked quickly at her in fear. "You didn't!"

"I had to. He asked for *you.* He didn't come to my door to see me; he wanted *you.* I just happened to be the one to answer the door and get in his way."

"I'm so sorry."

"You already said that. It's okay. None of this is your fault."

Rose hung her head again.

"I'm going to finish dinner. We're having spaghetti, your favorite," Abby said. "Why don't we stop talking about this, and you think about what happened, and what I said about testifying?"

Rose nodded her head and Abby returned to the stove. Nothing more was said about testifying that evening.

HAIRCUT AND HIGHLIGHTS

The next day was Saturday, so a leisure morning was enjoyed by both women. They drank their coffee slowly, unlike on a weekday morning. They hadn't been up long when they heard a soft knock on the door. Abby looked through the peephole, like she should have done the day before. Seeing that it was Mark in his uniform, she opened the door.

"Good morning," he said.

"Good morning."

"I just wanted to check on you after what happened yesterday," he said, looking handsome, despite his puffy lip.

"Come in. This is my roommate, Rose," she said, motioning to the couch. Rose nodded in response. "Would you like some coffee? It's the least I can do after yesterday."

"No, I'm on my way to work. Maybe another time when I'm not in a rush?"

"Of course. Any time you're so inclined, drop in."

"I'll do that."

"Thank you again for rescuing me," she said with a smile.

"Any time. My pleasure." He smiled back at her. "Okay, well, I really do have to get to work. I don't have much excuse for being late when the station is just across the street," he laughed.

"I guess not," she said, smiling up at him. "Have a good day."

"I will, thanks." And he was gone.

Abby turned from the door and rejoined Rose on the couch. "Nice guy."

"Yeah. He likes you."

"You think so?" Abby asked.

"Oh, yeah, he likes you all right. Why wouldn't he? You're gorgeous." Rose studied her coffee before speaking further. "I've been thinking about what you said about testifying."

Abby looked closely at her face. "Any new thoughts?"

Rose's eyes met Abby's. "Yes. I've decided I need to testify.

That guy is a bad dude. He could easily kill someone else. Like me."

"Oh, Rose, that makes me happy," she said. "It's the right thing to do. And I agree, he didn't come looking for you to say hi. He wants to kill you."

"I know. But the code on the street is survival. Any way you can. You don't go against that stuff." Rose held both hands around her cup—an act of hanging on.

"You are no longer on the street, Rose. All that is behind you. Gone forever," she stated with a wave of her hand. "You owe nothing to that man. He is a murderer who could have killed someone else by now. He needs to be behind bars, where he can't hurt anyone else."

"I agree; I really do. I will testify," Rose said with an affirmative nod. "But first, I have to tell the police."

FORTY

ABBY CALLED the police station and asked to speak to Sergeant Pardon. She was transferred to his extension quickly.

"Sergeant Pardon," he said abruptly.

"Hi, this is Abby," she said, hesitating.

"Did you stumble across more spit?" he asked.

She wasn't sure if he was attempting a joke or being serious. "No, but the guy matching that spit attempted to kill me yesterday in my apartment. He's been arrested."

"Yeah, I was just reviewing the officer's report." He sounded more involved now. "I see you were unharmed."

She took a deep breath. "Yes, just shook up. But there's more."

"Go on."

"Rose saw that man kill her boyfriend. She knows him and wants to make a report about what she witnessed."

"I see. And she's living with you now."

"How did you know?"

Jack chuckled. "I know everything that happens in my patch. What do you think snitches are for?"

"Then you know Rose didn't return to the street and has a

job now. She's rebuilding her life. Seems I remember saying previously she had potential." Abby felt some satisfaction saying those words.

"You did."

"Anyway, she wants to report what she saw."

"Can she come to the station?" he asked.

"Yes. She's right here. When do you want to see her?"

"Is now too soon?" he asked in all seriousness.

Abby grinned. *So impatient.* "I'm sure she can come in shortly. Within the hour. How is that?"

"Great. I'll look for her." Jack hung up without saying anything else.

"Now, it's up to you," she told Rose.

"I know. I'll get dressed and tell him what he wants to know." She rose from the couch and walked into her bedroom to dress.

"I can make some eggs and toast while you dress," Abby said, raising her voice.

"That would be great," Rose called back.

Thirty minutes later, Rose was heading out the door to do her duty as a citizen and human being. She was apprehensive, but despite her previous loyalties, Rose knew what she had to do. In order to be a functioning, responsible person, Rose had to snitch. This wasn't her preference, but it really was the right thing to do. If she could get that man permanently incarcerated, she had to do it. *He tried to kill Abby!* That thought made her shudder. If it hadn't been for the neighbor, she would have returned home to the apartment after work to find her friend, the only person to care about her, dead. No, that was too much. He was a dangerous man. He had to be stopped, loyalties be damned.

Rose squared her shoulders as she entered the police station,

HAIRCUT AND HIGHLIGHTS

prepared to give a report of what she had witnessed months ago.

Abby and Ivy were consulting over a woman's hair condition when George came into the salon, carrying the baby. All the women oohed and awed over the infant, delivering a variety of compliments. Some asked to hold Luna, others just wanted to coo to the little darling.

"She's growing so much," Abby said, adjusting a strap on the baby's shoulder. "So precious!"

The little girl had the beginnings of curly blonde hair, tiny wisps barely covering her scalp. Her big blue eyes followed everyone and everything that moved, and then she laughed over what she saw.

Ivy looked over at George, holding the baby. "You bringing her around for everyone to see?"

"Yeah. I'm on lunch break, so I thought I'd give everyone a thrill," he said with a proud papa grin. "Mrs. York didn't mind. This gives her a little break."

"I think it's wonderful that Mrs. York is still caring for the baby, even though you've moved out," Abby told them.

"It is. Luna loves her. And we love Mrs. York," Ivy said.

"Ditto," George said.

Sonia broke away from her client as soon as she had her settled under the dryer. "Ah, an angel," she said, cooing at the baby. "Look at cute jumper! Darling."

Ivy came over to Luna and gave her some love. "Luna Tuna." She gathered the baby in her arms. "Yes, mama's little Luna Tuna."

Abby chuckled over the nickname.

"Okay, give her back. I gotta drop off Luna at Mrs. York's place and get back to work," George said, reaching for the baby.

"Bye, Luna Tuna." Ivy waved as they went out the door. "Mama will see you soon."

The next time the bells jangled above the door, Rose walked into the salon.

"Hey, Rose," said Abby, smiling at her roommate.

"I think I need a haircut," she said. "But only the special kind that you give."

Abby laughed. "All right, give me ten and I'll snip you."

Ten minutes later, Rose was shampooed and sitting in Abby's chair. Abby was eager to know what had happened at the police station. "Tell me everything. Did Jack treat you okay?"

"He was all business. Totally respectful."

Abby was glad to hear Jack treated Rose with respect after the disparaging things he'd said about homeless people. Rose was a testament that the homeless could turn their lives around.

"And it went well?"

"Yes. The guy I know as Shep, the police were well aware of. He had ties to organized crime, I was told. He got kicked out and ended up homeless. So, I guess he was asserting his so-called authority on the homeless people, doing his deeds like he did before." Rose shrugged as Abby snipped away at her length. "The sergeant said he'll be arraigned tomorrow and won't get any bond. He's not going anywhere."

"That's a relief. For me, for you. He belongs behind bars," Abby said, remembering how menacing he was. Murder and attempted murder. He was going away for life, she guessed.

When Abby was done blow-drying her hair, she turned Rose around in the chair to face the mirror.

"Amazing. My roomie is the most amazing hair stylist," Rose said, a big smile across her face. "Everything in my world has changed for the good. How'd I get so lucky?"

"Maybe God had something to do with it," Abby suggested.

"I'm beginning to think you're right."

When Abby returned home from work, she practically dragged herself up the two flights of stairs. Her feet were tired, and her hands felt cramped from holding scissors for hours. As she came to the top of the second staircase, there stood Mark. He wasn't in uniform, but rather blue jeans and a casual tee with Daytona Beach Fest printed across his chest in blue.

"Hey," he said with a smile.

"Hey, yourself."

"I thought you might be coming home soon."

"Yes, I'm right on time."

"I bet you're tired."

"Every bit of me is screaming 'sit down.'"

He chuckled. "I can handle that."

"Handle what?"

"You're tired, but I'm rested. Had the whole day off." He smiled, his teeth glowing in the dim light. "So, I fixed the best chili you've ever eaten, and you're invited to join me for a feast destined to invigorate the senses."

"Really?" Abby couldn't believe what she was hearing.

"Yes, really," he said, reaching for her arm. "Follow me to your dining delight. I have this great bread recipe, too, so I thought that would go well with the chili. You do like chili?"

"Yes, of course. Who doesn't?" she smiled up into his face as she walked alongside him. "What a treat."

"And there are many more treats to come," he said, opening the door to his apartment ... and all the possibilities that could blossom from a simple chili dinner.

The delightful scent of baking bread immediately tickled her nose. She also noticed that Mark smelled pretty tasty himself ... *Lucky me!*

ABOUT THE AUTHOR

Janie Owens is traditionally and self-published, sometimes under the name Elizabeth Owens. Llewellyn Worldwide published five nonfiction instructional books with the second winning Best Biographical/Personal Book from the Coalition of Visionary Resources in 2002. The Next Chapter Publishing has released three novels in the *50-Plus Condo* series, *The Murder*, *The Daughter*, and *The Couples*, with number four in the series currently in creation. *Haircut and Highlights: Daytona Beach Mysteries*, Book 1, begins another exciting series set in romantic, beautiful Florida.

Some of Janie's interests besides writing are reading, painting, and travel. Janie and her husband Vincent have a houseful of fur-babies. Both cats and dogs (mostly) reside peacefully in their large central Florida home. However, if you've ever owned Chihuahuas, you know that quiet is not often heard. Bina and Peewee keep life interesting for the cats.

To learn more about Janie Owens and discover more Next Chapter authors, visit our website at www.nextchapter.pub.